HAPPILY FOR NOW

ILLUSTRATIONS BY
KELLY MURPHY

HAPPILY
FOR NOW

KELLY JONES

ALFRED A. KNOPF

NEW YORK

FOR THOSE WHO WANT TO HELP,
AND THOSE WHO WORK TO MAKE THINGS BETTER.

AND FOR MANDY AND NANCY, THE BEST FAIRY
GODPEOPLE THIS STORY COULD HAVE.

HAPPILY
FOR NOW

1

THINGS ARE A lot simpler in fairy tales. I mean, when you read about some girl going around covered in ashes who gets treated way worse than her stepsisters, it's pretty clear somebody should get that girl some help.

Then again, who knows what she thought when she woke up every morning? Maybe she thought, *Well, things could be better, but they could be a lot worse, too.* (Trust me, they could—and in lots of fairy tales they are. If you've ever read the original versions, you know they get gruesome fast.) Maybe she was glad her stepmother was bugging her stepsisters instead of her about what they wore or why they didn't go out and find someone rich to marry. Maybe she was okay with doing her own thing.

You get used to what's normal for you. You might think it's not that big a deal when Mom doesn't bring food home, because at least the cupboards aren't as bare as Old Mother Hubbard's. It doesn't really matter if she doesn't pay a bill and the lights in your apartment don't work for a couple of days, because nobody had electricity in any of those stories, and they got by. And if your mom doesn't come home when she's supposed to, well, she probably didn't get turned into a swan or fall asleep for a hundred years. She's probably just really late. Again.

But even in our everyday world, someone could be keeping an eye out, watching to see if you need some help. If you do need help, and if you're lucky, you get a fairy godperson. Ms. Davis is mine. She's very good at her job.

I don't remember when I first met Ms. Davis—years and years ago. She works for a community program that helps families get through their problems and find support when they need it. Sometimes, when things are going pretty well, I don't see her much. But this wasn't really one of those times.

When my mom told me I had to go stay with relatives I don't even know, I called Ms. Davis. I keep one of her business cards by the phone, and another with my important stuff, so I always know how to reach her.

As soon as I heard her voice, I felt calmer. She suggested we get together the next day and talk, and I agreed.

When I got out of school, she was waiting in her old blue Toyota, right where she said she'd be. I ran over, and when she got out and gave me one of her big squeezy hugs, I knew things would be okay.

She let go of me and opened the trunk so I could put

my backpack inside while we walked. "Shall we go to the track?"

"Sure," I said. Ms. Davis's doctor says it's a good idea for her to get some exercise. But she gets bored doing laps on her own, and I don't mind walking with her while we talk. This way, we help each other get things done.

I stayed quiet while we walked down the street to the track, filled up our water bottles, and put our sunscreen on. I didn't really know what to say.

Nobody who saw us would think we were working on fairy-godperson stuff. There weren't any carriages or pumpkins or princesses—just the springy brown rubber track, marked off in walking lanes and running lanes, with a few rows of empty bleachers and a chain-link fence. But when I looked at Ms. Davis, I didn't just see her hot pink walking shoes and her black braids and her dark brown skin and her look that said, *You called me—remember?* I saw someone who knows how to make things better. Even if I've never seen her with a magic wand.

But she can only help me if I tell her what's going on. She has a lot to say about those fairy godpeople in stories who decide what's best for other people before talking it out. She says that's no way to behave, wand or no wand.

I took a deep breath and looked at my sneakers. "I don't want to live with people I don't know. I want to stay here with my mom."

"I can understand that," Ms. Davis said. "Change isn't

easy for me, either. But when you gathered your courage last week, you told your mom you wished she'd stop waiting around for things to get better and start working on her addiction. Is that still what you want?"

Ms. Davis believes in calling things what they are. You don't fix things by pretending they're something else. She let the question hang in the air between us as we followed the curve in the track.

"Yeah. But *I* could help her," I said at last. "I know she has to work on her problems. But who's going to look out for her if I'm not around?"

"That sounds like an important question to ask her," Ms. Davis said. "But let me ask you this: If your mom says she's found a program with people she trusts, people who can help her work on those problems, only she needs to be able to give it her full attention, what would you say?"

I gulped down some water. "I wouldn't distract her," I said quietly. "I know how to take care of myself. It would be like I wasn't even here."

Ms. Davis gave me a long look.

I could see my own face reflected in the mirrors of her

 sunglasses: two tiny white faces under a lot of red hair, looking scared and sad.

"And would that be fair to *you*?"

I wanted to say yes. But Ms. Davis says you shouldn't say the first thing that comes into your head without thinking about it. That's definitely true for fairy tales, too. That's how people start out with wishes and end up with sausages stuck to their noses. (Look it up, if you don't believe me.)

"This isn't how my wish was supposed to work." My voice felt as small and as scared as my reflection.

"You and those stories." Ms. Davis shook her head and sighed. "Fiona, we've talked about this. It takes more than wishing to make things better."

My voice got louder. I hated that I couldn't stop it. "I told her I wished she'd do what moms are supposed to! I didn't tell her to send me away!" I rubbed my sleeve over my eyes. If I'd just kept quiet, none of this would have happened. A mean little voice in my head said, *If you were really my fairy godmother, you would have made my wish turn out right.* But I kept my lips tight together and didn't let that voice out. I know wishes aren't that simple.

Ms. Davis stopped walking. She turned and put her hands on my shoulders. "Take a breath, Fiona. I need you to listen to me," she said quietly. "This situation is not your fault. You didn't cause your mom's addiction, and you can't control it, any more than you could any other disease. Right?"

I was crying now, too hard to answer, so I just nodded. She got her pocket tissues out and handed me one. Fairy godmothers are always prepared.

And they have a lot to say, even when you don't really

want to hear it. "Breathe with me for a moment." Her voice was calm.

I did, crushing the soggy tissue into a ball. We stood there and just breathed until I could look up and listen again.

Ms. Davis nodded, satisfied. "I'm so proud of you, Fiona. You told your mom what you needed to tell her. I hear you. This next step on the journey isn't what you hoped for. But everybody's got their own job to do. Yours was to tell her what you were holding inside you—where you want that journey to end up. Now hers is to figure out the best way to get herself there. You don't get to decide that for her. And when she asks you for some help, I'd like you to stop and consider whether that's help you're willing to give."

"Of course I can help her!" I said. "That's what I've been telling you!"

Ms. Davis raised her eyebrow above her sunglasses. "Even if the help she asks for—the help she says she needs right now to make things better for both of you—is to give her some space while she's at this program?"

We walked a whole lap in silence while I thought about that.

"I still want to help her," I said finally.

She smiled at me and squeezed my shoulder. "I'm glad to hear it. You know how hard it is to ask for help. I hope you're proud of her for asking."

I nodded. Just because she was right didn't mean I had to be happy about it.

"Are you ready to give her the help she asked for, instead of the help you'd like to give?"

"I guess so."

We walked in silence for a while, until we passed the bleachers again.

Then Ms. Davis gave me one of her special fairy-godmother looks, the kind that can see all the way through you. Fairy godpeople have to be able to do that, or how are they going to figure out what you wish for in your most secret of hearts? "This is a lot to be dealing with, Fiona. How are you feeling about it?"

I took a deep, slow breath, all the way in, and then let it all the way out. "Pretty mad, I guess. But I'm ready to focus on the positive now." There's no point trying to hide anything from a really good fairy godmother like Ms. Davis. But I've learned I can change the subject sometimes.

Ms. Davis nodded very slowly, like she knew exactly what I was doing but had decided to let me get away with it, for now. "One positive I see is that your mom is ready to get some help. She needs some new tools, and it will be much easier for her to focus on what she's learning if she knows you're safe with family. I do wish this part was easier on you, though. What positives do you see?"

I held up a finger. "One: the relatives I'll be staying with definitely need some help."

Ms. Davis's eyebrows went up. "And you know this how?"

"Because I read the email Great-Aunt Alta sent Mom,"

I said. "Yeah, she said I could stay with them. 'Anything for Robert's grandchild' was how she put it. That's me. But then it was all doom this and gloom that, and oh, by the way, they're probably going to lose their bakery and move, but not until fall, so whatever."

Ms. Davis lowered her sunglasses and gave me a look over the top. "When did reading other people's emails without their permission become okay?"

"When my mom decided to send me away to live with people like that," I shot back, folding my arms. Then I stopped myself and took another deep breath. I was focusing on the positive, after all. "Anyway, it proved they have a lot of problems."

"And this is a positive because . . . ?" Ms. Davis waited, still looking me right in the eye.

I put my chin up. "How am I going to learn to help people the way you do unless they have problems? I know you think I'm too young, and I should just enjoy myself. But I can't. Not when I'm going to stay with people I don't even know. If Mom has to concentrate on learning her stuff, fine. I'll focus on learning mine, too. It's the perfect time to start my fairy-godperson training. What else is there for me to do there? Wait around for my happily-ever-after, like I'm some princess?"

Ms. Davis opened her mouth, all ready to argue, like she does every time I bring up anything about fairy godpeople. She always says that's not her job at all; her job is helping people make their own lives better, and that takes work, not wishes. I've tried to explain that sometimes hard work isn't enough—people need magic. You can't fix a curse like my mom's with stuff like deep breaths. But that's one area where we just don't agree.

Then Ms. Davis stopped herself and took a minute to think. She looked at me hard, like she was seeing me with her magic as well as with her eyes. "Maybe it *is* the right time for you to start learning a few things," she said slowly. "Fairy-godmother training, huh?"

I shook my head. I'd thought this all through a long time ago. "I might need to help people who are older than I am, so why would I call myself their mother? That's just weird. I'm going to be a fairy god*person*."

Ms. Davis gave that some thought. "And what kind of training did you have in mind?"

"You know—how to help people focus on the positive, and figure out what they wish for, and speak up about it. And how to make it happen, without getting all discouraged." I hesitated. "How to grant wishes, too. But I guess that part comes later."

Ms. Davis nodded, still thinking. "I suppose I could send you some lessons. But if you truly want to learn to help people, you're going to have to put the work in and pay attention to what's really going on. A helper—or a fairy godperson, for that matter—who barges forward without paying attention is worse than no help at all."

I grinned and hugged her. "Deal." Ms. Davis doesn't mess around when it comes to important stuff. She sets her expectations high, so you'd better start working to meet them. But I knew I could do it. I had to, or who was going to help my mom? I'd let her try it her way first, because that was the help she asked me for. And then I'd come home, ready to really help her.

"Good," Ms. Davis said, sliding her sunglasses back up in place and starting to walk again. "I'll send your first lesson in an email before you leave. When you get there and get settled, you can write and tell me how things are going. Now, back to this world for a moment. I'd like to hear more about how you're getting there, and if there are any other things we should talk about, like what to pack, or what might help you feel more comfortable there."

We did three more laps while I answered all her questions and talked through the things she wanted to talk about, like who my temporary fairy godperson was going to be for the summer. He's not my official helper, just a friend of hers with the same training she has. But she said that I could call him, the same way I could call or email her, if I wanted or needed to.

"How are you doing with all this now?" Ms. Davis asked.

I shrugged. I didn't really want to think about any of it. Not about packing up my stuff or leaving our apartment behind. Not about hugging my mom goodbye. "I'm excited about my training," I said finally. I knew she'd just wait until I answered. "It feels weird to be excited when I'm still mad and worried and sad."

"Feelings are complicated," Ms. Davis said. "But it's good to see any positives and have the fun you can, even when other parts are hard. I've got my own mixed-up feelings, you know. I'm glad your mom is getting some help. But I'm going to miss seeing you this summer. You know how to reach me anytime."

"I know," I told her as we rounded the curve again. Ms. Davis helps lots of kids, not just me. And my relatives live an hour away. But she always answers my emails and returns my messages as soon as she can, and if I ever need her, she finds a way to help. It's what she does.

And now I was finally going to learn to do it, too.

Dear Fiona,

I'm guessing you might be feeling a little unsure about things, settling into a new place with your relatives for the summer. I want you to know I'm proud of you for helping your mom, even if it's not the way you wanted to. Even if it is a little scary. And I'm glad you spoke up and told me how I could help you this summer. You're right—this is important stuff to learn.

Sometimes people think that helpers like me have all the power—that we're born with a magic wand or something. That's not true. Any magic we have, we have to learn, and that learning takes work.

So here's your first lesson.

FAIRY-GODPERSON TRAINING: LESSON 1

1. Find someone who seems unhappy.
2. Observe what's really going on.
3. Encourage them to make one small change.

You'll notice that this isn't about fixing everything for them. If you do that, how are they going to learn how to make things better for themselves the next time something goes wrong? We live in the real world here. Stuff happens, and we can't stop it. All we can do is to try and help each other make things better.

It isn't about jumping in before you really understand what's going on, either. Helping people takes time and effort. Sometimes the parts that are hard for them aren't the parts we expect, and sometimes their goals aren't what we'd pick for them. Remember, we only get to live our own lives, not theirs.

Take your time with this lesson—don't just rush through it. You might even decide to try it with more than one person, if the opportunity presents itself. And since I'm your teacher here, let me know how it's going and what you're learning. I want to hear about what works well and what could be better next time. After all, you can learn just as much from your mistakes as you can from your successes.

Let me know how you're doing, too. And say hi to Mr. Rivera for me. He's a good friend, and he has a lot of experience helping people, too. I'm glad he'll be there for you.

Sincerely,
Nia Davis

2

IT WAS DARK the night my mom took me to my relatives'
creepy old house, in some town called Cold Hope. It was way
darker than our city ever gets. I couldn't see much. Maybe
my eyes were too full to see anything anyway.

I don't remember coming up the path through the over-
grown garden or knocking on the big black front door. All I
remember is clutching my mom's hand, tight in mine, like I
was a little kid again.

It hadn't felt real on the drive. Sometimes magic waits
until the last minute to save people in stories. But when the
front door opened and we went inside, my heart started
pounding so hard I couldn't pay attention to anything else.
Mom was talking to some people—my relatives, I guess. But
I couldn't focus on her words. It was too much. I couldn't
do this.

I flung my arms around her and buried my face. I felt

her squeeze my shoulders for a moment. When I looked up, there were tears running down her face, too. But she took my hand and pulled me gently along as we walked around the house.

It felt like everything was roaring and swirling around me, like I was stuck in a tornado halfway to Oz. Someone kept talking and talking, pointing stuff out, but I couldn't listen. Mom tried to ask me something, but I couldn't answer. I felt like I couldn't even breathe. She squeezed my hand.

When we got back to where we started, Mom said something—and then we were outside, and I could breathe again. We could go home.

But she knelt down and pulled me close. "I love you, sweetie," she whispered, her arms around me. "More than anything. You know that, right?"

And I knew we weren't going home. I nodded. I wanted to beg her to take me with her. But I was crying too hard to get the words out. I knew this was goodbye. All I could do was hug her harder.

Until she pulled away and left, disappearing into the night. Like someone whose curse had caught up with her.

I WOKE UP IN A BED I DIDN'T RECOGNIZE, IN A SMALL WHITE ROOM with a sloped ceiling. I sat right up, heart pounding. Something rang, like a bell, somewhere nearby. I jumped out of bed and then stopped. No one was yelling or breaking any-thing or crying.

It's not going to be easy, Ms. Davis said in my memory. *But I know you can do this, Fiona.*

Slowly, I sat down on the bed as the sound faded away. I didn't want this to be real. But there was my backpack, and there were my boxes, with everything I might need. The blankets were scratchy under my fingers but warm, and the room was clean.

The light through the small window looked gray and dim. It was early, I thought. Really early. But I didn't want to stay in bed, trying to fall back asleep. Not when I could feel my mind going around and around like a hamster wheel.

Just take it one step at a time, Ms. Davis advised in my mind.

I took a deep breath, got up, and opened the box I'd decorated. There was my first-day outfit, packed right on top, with my hairbrush and everything else I needed to get ready. Get dressed. . . . Wash my face. . . . Brush my hair. . . . Fill up my backpack with what I might need for the day. I felt my heart calm a little more with every step I checked off my list.

Then I read through Lesson 1 once more. I'd printed it out and kept it safe, along with the money Mom had given me in case I needed something this summer, and her email address, and Ms. Davis's business card, and Mr. Rivera's phone number.

Right. Fairy godpeople did not wait around in attics wondering what to do. They got to work. I put on my backpack and went downstairs to figure out where things were and find my relatives.

The kitchen was plain and kind of worn. But it was clean. Gray light came in through the window over the sink. A frying pan swung slowly back and forth on the pot rack overhead.

Great-Aunt Alta, my mom's aunt, was standing by the sink. She was tall and thin, with pale skin and white hair and fierce dark eyes. Her long black dress made me think of wicked witches. But you can't tell that kind of thing about a person just by looking. "Welcome, Robert's grandchild," she said.

"My name's Fiona," I told her, trying to smile.

She didn't bother to smile back.

My stomach wobbled. Ms. Davis was wrong—I couldn't do this. Then I remembered the first part of Lesson 1: *Find someone who seems unhappy.* Great-Aunt Alta did look like someone who could use a fairy godperson, even if she turned out to be a wicked witch. After all, there are just as many witches as princesses in fairy tales, and who looks out for them? I hadn't really thought about it before, but it seemed like they just got forgotten about. No wonder they met bad ends.

An old guy with wild white hair appeared in the doorway: Great-Uncle Timothy. He was Great-Aunt Alta's brother and my mom's uncle. He was tall and thin, too, but he didn't look wicked, just sad. Like a king whose kingdom was having hard times. He tried to smile, I think, but it didn't really work. Maybe he'd forgotten how? I'd never read a fairy tale about a king with a fairy godperson. But a lot of them were written back in the days when people only helped princesses, and stuff like that was not fair. It doesn't mean we shouldn't be fair now that we know better. Great-Uncle Timothy definitely looked like he could use some help.

Aunt Becky followed him in. She was Great-Aunt Alta's daughter and Great-Uncle Timothy's niece and Mom's cousin. She said I could call her my aunt instead of my first cousin once removed, because that was kind of a mouthful. She was around Mom's age, but she looked tired and kind of faded, too, like a princess whose fairy godmother never turned up to help her. She looked like she never expected anything good to happen again, and like having me there wasn't going to change that.

I decided right away that I would prove her wrong. Because I'm not some princess who's going to wait around for help. I'm a fairy-godperson-in-training. I make my own help.

"Yogurt is all that remains," Great-Aunt Alta said. She sounded like she was telling a ghost story or talking about the end of the world. She'd fit right in with the Goth kids at school, if she wasn't an old lady. She scooped some plain yogurt into a bowl and put it down on the table.

But I wasn't here for her doom and gloom, and I wasn't going to eat plain yogurt, either. When we talked through it all, Mom and Ms. Davis had gone over Great-Aunt Alta's house rules and explained things very clearly: My relatives had agreed to provide what I needed, and I didn't have to act like a guest in their house. I could help myself when I got hungry, the same way I did at home, within reason. (Meaning no dessert for breakfast or anything like that.)

I knew how to dress up my yogurt without turning it into dessert, no problem. I opened the fridge, found a jar of blackberry jam, and mixed some into my yogurt. Much better. "Thanks," I told Great-Aunt Alta.

"The jam will not last," she said sadly, watching me.

"Well, yeah—someone needs to eat it or it'll get moldy and go to waste," I told her. "Then you have to buy more." I didn't expect to have to help her with that kind of stuff. That's just basic. "How's your morning going?"

She didn't answer right away, just stared out the kitchen window. "Life is filled with suffering," she said at last.

I swallowed a spoonful of yogurt. That was a bigger problem than I wanted to tackle today. But all I had to do was find one small thing that might help. "Do you want some jam in your yogurt?"

She just shook her head, like jam wouldn't make any difference at all.

Then I noticed something. Great-Aunt Alta's face looked calm and sad, but her fingers were tapping something out on the counter. Something really complicated. "Do you know Morse code?" I asked her.

She looked down at her hands and stopped. "No."

"Do you want to learn it? So you can become a spy or something?" I didn't know if people could become spies when they were as old as she was. I'd have to do some research and find out.

"No." Great-Aunt Alta trailed out of the kitchen, putting an end to that conversation.

It was annoying, but there wasn't any point in chasing after her and demanding that she tell me how to help. So I reminded myself I had the whole summer and let it go. For now.

Besides, I had other people to help.

Somewhere in the house a clock started bonging. "We're going to the bakery," Aunt Becky said softly, rinsing out her yogurt bowl. "We'll be back later."

Right. In her email, Great-Aunt Alta had said something about "losing the bakery." This sounded like fairy-godperson work to me. Time to find out more. "What does your bakery make?" I asked.

"Blueberry muffins, chocolate chip cookies, oatmeal-raisin cookies, chocolate cupcakes with yellow sprinkles, white cupcakes with pink sprinkles, and banana bread," Aunt Becky said, and sighed.

"With chocolate chips or without?" I asked.

Aunt Becky blinked. "What?"

"Do you make banana bread with chocolate chips or without?" I asked patiently.

Great-Aunt Alta appeared in the doorway. "We make it the same way it's always been made."

"Do you work there, too?" I asked.

Great-Aunt Alta frowned and disappeared again.

I figured I knew what that meant. And I definitely wasn't going to stay in a big spooky old house with Great-Aunt Alta moping around and clocks bonging like we were in a horror movie. "I'll come with you," I told Aunt Becky.

Great-Uncle Timothy looked nervous, and Aunt Becky tried to talk me out of it. But she wasn't very good at trying to convince someone who'd already made up her mind. You'd think she'd have had plenty of practice, with Great-Aunt Alta around. But no.

I GOT A BETTER LOOK AT THE TOWN OF COLD HOPE AS WE DROVE TO the bakery. Not that I could see much. Lots of trees, some houses, a few short buildings. No skyscrapers or stadiums or museums. Not even many bus stops or apartment buildings. Or people. We passed a school that looked empty (since it was summer), two churches that looked empty (since it was Monday), and a bank that only looked sort of empty. There were open parking places everywhere.

It didn't make me feel very hopeful. But it wasn't actually cold, either, since it was June. I wondered if towns needed fairy godpeople, too, and if this one's would give it a new name. What would I call it?

"Here we are," Aunt Becky said, pulling into a small parking lot and stopping.

I unbuckled my seat belt, got out, and had a look. The bakery was a plain little yellow box of a store, with STARKE BROS. BAKERY painted in big faded blue letters across the top.

"Who are the Starke Bros.?" I asked.

"It's short for 'Starke Brothers,'" Aunt Becky told me. "The bakery began with my grandfather and his brothers, long before I was born. Then it passed to my mother's brothers, Uncle Timothy and Uncle Robert. Uncle Robert was your grandfather. He died a couple years after it opened."

"Did he like to bake?" I asked. Mom never really talked about her dad. She was a little kid when he died. "Did your dad work here, too?"

"No, no—my dad wasn't a Starke," Aunt Becky said. "He was a scientist. He moved to Antarctica when I was very young."

"For science?" I asked. I didn't know that people actually lived in Antarctica. But what else was there to do there?

"I suppose. All Mother will say was that he insisted on peace and quiet."

"Is she so gloomy all the time because her brother died and your dad left? Wait, did Great-Aunt Alta ever work here? Why isn't it 'Starke Brothers and Sister'? And why didn't you change it to 'Starke Uncle and Niece' when you started working here?"

Aunt Becky sighed and unlocked the door.

I looked at Great-Uncle Timothy, but he just stared up at the letters, like he was seeing them for the first time in years. He didn't talk much. Neither of them was going to make my job easy. But that probably made them extra-good practice.

The inside of the bakery wasn't fancy or anything. There was a long counter with a cash register and a couple of glass cases that divided the room into two parts, separating the customers from the bakery kitchen. A sign hung over the counter. It was a list of the cookies and things Aunt Becky had mentioned. Some of the sticker letters were so old they were falling off.

Aunt Becky walked back behind the counter, into the kitchen, and I followed her. I'd never been in a bakery kitchen before. The left wall had ovens—not just one or two but four, all in a row, next to a big metal sink. The back wall had a long, long counter, with cabinets underneath. I wondered what was inside. Sprinkles in every color? More cookie-cutter shapes than I could imagine?

In the middle of the kitchen stood an enormous mixer. It was taller than me. Next to it was an island made out of even more cabinets, with a counter on top. I opened one of the cabinets, just to see. It was packed full of muffin pans and muffin papers.

The right wall had glass-front cupboards that went all the way up to the ceiling. They were full of baking ingredients: flour and sugar and spices and a container of chocolate chips that looked almost too heavy for me to lift. There were hooks full of aprons and a huge fridge and a door marked EMPLOYEES ONLY. I decided I was practically an employee and opened the door. Nobody stopped me. It led to a short hallway with a bathroom and a locked door at the end. It didn't look like a treasure vault or anything, though. It looked like the janitor's closet at school.

Still, this place had possibilities, I decided as I came back into the kitchen. A fairy godperson could definitely get something done here.

Aunt Becky put on one of the aprons, tying it behind her back like she'd done it a million times before. So I put one on, too. It hung down to the floor, and I couldn't figure out how to tie it when I couldn't see it. But Aunt Becky pulled it up and tied a knot in the strap at the back of my neck so it wasn't so long. Then she belted it up at the waist, wrapping the strings around so I could tie it in front instead.

"Thanks," I said as she put a thing like a shower cap over her hair, washed her hands, and pulled on plastic gloves. She nodded and handed me my own shower cap and gloves. I tucked all my hair inside the cap, just like she had, before I washed my hands and before I put my gloves on.

"Can I help?" I asked as Aunt Becky started measuring and dumping things into the enormous mixer bowl.

She shook her head. "Too dangerous." She adjusted a dial on the side and pushed a button. The Enormous Mixer of Danger started up, grinding away.

Maybe if it really got going and fell over on top of me, it might crush me, though that seemed pretty unlikely. Whatever. I could find another job for myself.

"I'll put the muffin papers in the pans for you," I told her. That would buy me some time to figure out something more interesting to do.

She looked a little surprised, but I guess she couldn't think of any way that could be dangerous. She dug a big box of white muffin papers and a pan out of the cupboard and put them on the counter for me.

For a while, everything was quiet, except for the mixer grinding away and the rustle of muffin papers. Great-Uncle Timothy poured water into both sides of a coffee machine and pushed a button. The smell of coffee filled the room.

I wasn't actually there to put papers in muffin pans, though. I was there to do fairy-godperson work.

Aunt Becky seemed unhappy, but I didn't know what was wrong. I was supposed to be observing what was really going on. But I didn't see why I couldn't ask a few questions. I thought about the questions Ms. Davis and I liked to talk about, and picked a good one. "What's your favorite kind of cookie?"

See, a question like that seems like no big deal, so it doesn't make you nervous. You can't get it wrong. But cookies can tell you a lot about a person. For instance, my favorites are oatmeal with chocolate chips. Ms. Davis says they're a lot like me: you might not notice right away that they're something special, but once you do, you'll never make that mistake again. Ms. Davis's favorites are these spicy molasses cookies she makes. She says they're just like her: they keep getting better with age, and people always remember them.

Great-Uncle Timothy didn't say anything. Maybe he needed to think about it, or maybe he was still feeling shy around me. Or maybe he just didn't like to talk that much.

But Aunt Becky answered right away, like she'd been waiting her whole life for someone to ask. "Pistachio-oatmeal bars with raspberry jam." She folded her arms, like she was daring me to make something of it.

"I've never had those," I said, wondering what they said about a person. "Are you going to make them next?"

Her shoulders slumped, and she let her arms fall back down by her sides. "We only make chocolate chip and oatmeal-raisin. Mother says that's all people want."

I looked out at the empty bakery. No one had come in, not even for coffee. "What people?"

"Business is bad," Aunt Becky said with a sigh. "Mother says we can't afford to try something new. Not now, when we might lose the bakery."

"That doesn't make any sense," I told her. "My fairy— I mean, my . . . uh . . . friend—Ms. Davis says that if what you're doing isn't working for you, you have to try something else, not keep doing more of the same."

Aunt Becky just shook her head and sighed again.

I put the last paper in the muffin pan. So was Aunt Becky unhappy because the bakery was in trouble? Or maybe because she baked the same boring stuff every day? I wasn't sure how to fix all that. But Lesson 1 just said to encourage her to make one small change.

"Can I try making your cookies?" I asked.

3

AUNT BECKY TURNED the Enormous Mixer of Danger off. She looked at me—really looked at me—like she was trying to figure out if she could trust me.

I didn't rush her, and I didn't push. I just waited as she scooped muffin batter into all the muffin papers.

But when she handed the pan to Great-Uncle Timothy, I asked, "Can I at least see the recipe?"

For a minute, I thought maybe she would just say no. We both watched Great-Uncle Timothy add three blueberries to the top of each muffin, in a little cluster design. He pushed them around with a toothpick until they were right where he wanted them.

When he was done, Aunt Becky slid the muffin pan into the first oven and set the timer.

Then, slowly, she went to the very last cabinet in the row. She knelt down, moved a pile of dish towels aside, and reached way back into the darkness, where I couldn't see.

When she stood up, she was holding a box. It was plain wood, nothing special. But she held it like it was her treasure chest. She flipped through the index cards inside, chose one, and handed it to me.

I read the recipe. It was a little like my mom's oatmeal-cookie recipe, except it called for pistachios instead of chocolate chips, and you put half the dough in a big pan, then jam on top, and then the other half of the dough, and then cut them up after they were baked instead of using a spoon to plop them on a cookie sheet. I never did that before. But I know how to measure and mix things, so how hard could it be?

When I looked up, Aunt Becky was watching me. Kind of like it was a test. Only she didn't look like the teacher—she looked like *she* was taking the test.

"Where's the pan?" I asked.

While she got it out, I found a bowl that wasn't Enormous Mixer of Danger–size. I looked in the tall cupboards for the chopped pistachios and the oats and one of the big jars of jam, and set out the measuring cups and spoons I was going to need. I lined everything up on the long counter in a way that made me happy. I like things to be organized. It makes me feel like I can get my work done without any unexpected problems getting in my way.

Aunt Becky brought me a big glass pan and a sheet of special paper called baking parchment. She showed me how to line the pan with it so the cookies wouldn't stick. You don't have to put butter on it or anything. Then I started measuring my ingredients.

The timer went off, loud in the quiet air, scaring me half to death. Slowly, Great-Uncle Timothy went over to the oven. He turned the pan around and set the timer again. Then he started washing the dirty dishes.

But Aunt Becky stayed right where she was, watching me.

I measured everything very carefully, and mixed it all together. Her face was kind of frowny, but she didn't look mad at me. Just concentrating, maybe. And maybe waiting? Hoping for something?

I dumped half the dough in the big glass pan and started pressing it down with a spoon, like the recipe said to.

"Let me show you a trick for that," Aunt Becky said. She took a drinking glass and used the bottom to flatten the dough. Then she handed the glass to me and watched as I did the rest of it. I was careful, and I squished it where I wanted it to go, so the whole thing ended up almost even. (I kind of wanted to remind Aunt Becky that her other cookies weren't going to make themselves, so she'd stop watching me and making me nervous. But that didn't seem like a fairy-godperson thing to do.)

Measuring and then spreading the jam was easy. Dumping the rest of the dough on top was harder, because I didn't want to mess up the jam underneath. Aunt Becky taught me how to take a spoonful of the crumbly dough and kind of shake it over the pan, so it scattered more evenly. She said it was okay if it wasn't completely even, because these were "rustic-style" cookies. But I pushed the topping around a little bit, very carefully, so you couldn't see any big patches of jam anymore.

Then Aunt Becky showed me how to turn one of the huge timers until it started ticking, like an alarm clock in a cartoon. We set it for half of the baking time, so we could turn the pan around in the oven and make sure it baked evenly. Aunt Becky said cookies that you're selling have to be as perfect as you can make them, not burned on the edges at all, and even though we couldn't sell these, because they weren't choco-late chip or oatmeal-raisin, I should still do it right.

While we waited, I got out another muffin pan and started to put the papers in.

"Not white papers," Aunt Becky said. "White papers are for blueberry muffins. Chocolate cupcakes have yellow papers."

I checked the clock. "Who wants cupcakes before eight in the morning?" I asked. "Shouldn't you make more muf-fins?"

She shook her head. "One batch of blueberry muffins, one batch of chocolate cupcakes with—"

"Yeah, I know," I said, cutting her off. These people were really not into mixing it up. Like, at all. "So, one pan with yellow papers. And one pan with pink for the other cupcakes?"

Aunt Becky nodded and started measuring ingredients into a bowl.

So I put the white papers back in the package and got out the yellow papers instead. The timer went off, startling me all over again.

"Muffins," Aunt Becky said, not moving. I could see that the timer over the oven with our cookies was still ticking.

Great-Uncle Timothy opened the first oven and pulled out the pan of muffins. After they'd cooled a little, he tipped them out onto a big wire rack on the counter. As he turned each one right side up, he arranged them into a pattern, like a wavy circle. Then he frowned at it, pulled one out, and re-arranged them some more to fill the gap. He brought me the muffin he'd pulled out on a napkin.

"Thanks," I said. I peeled off the paper and took a bite. The muffin was warm and sweet. But it didn't taste any different from the ones at the grocery store. I didn't know why anyone would bother to come buy one here.

Great-Uncle Timothy waited until Aunt Becky turned the mixer back on. Then he leaned over and whispered, "Banana bread with chocolate chips tomorrow." His voice was scratchy, like he hadn't used it in years.

I grinned at him. I hadn't pictured him as a rebel. But if he was up for it, so was I.

Finally, my cookies' second-half timer went off. Aunt Becky hovered over me as I put the oven mitts on and pulled out the pan. "Are these done?" I asked.

She closed her eyes and took a long sniff, like she could smell if they were done better than she could see it. They did smell amazing, nutty and oaty, fruity and sweet.

She nodded and told me to put the pan on a rack on the counter to cool. She went back to her chocolate cupcakes, and I put the pink papers in the next pan.

After Aunt Becky put the white-cupcake batter into the pink papers and popped them in the oven, she said the cookies were cool enough to cut up. Unfortunately, my cutting lines wiggled, and some of the cookies ended up a little bigger and some a little smaller. Worse still, the first one broke into three pieces when I tried to get it out of the pan.

I took a deep breath and reminded myself that it's okay to make mistakes as long as you learn something from them.

Aunt Becky glanced over at me and saw the broken cookie pieces. But she didn't frown. "That always happens with the first one," she told me. "It's another reason we can't sell them here. We can't waste ingredients like that."

I put the pieces on three small white napkins. I took the first one to Great-Uncle Timothy, who stopped rearranging muffins in the bakery case long enough to taste it. I watched him carefully.

When he put it in his mouth, his eyebrows shot straight up, like hairy white caterpillars jumping. He looked at Aunt

Becky, but he didn't say anything. Then he smiled. It was a small smile, but it was real: the first real smile since I got here. It gave me a warm feeling in my stomach. Like maybe things would be okay, even if they weren't perfect.

I gave the next piece to Aunt Becky, but she just set it down on the counter without really looking at it.

I tried not to be disappointed. Sometimes people don't notice right away when you do something nice for them. Sometimes you have to do your own thing and let people do theirs.

I took a bite of my piece.

I'd known for years I was an oatmeal-cookie-with-chocolate-chips kind of girl, with a brownie now and then. But this pistachio-oatmeal bar almost changed my mind. The sour-sweet jam and the buttery, nutty cookie, which was still warm . . . It made me smile, even though I still felt kind of sad.

Aunt Becky was watching me. Her hand reached out, almost like it was doing its own thing, and broke off a tiny piece of her cookie. She put it into her mouth and closed her eyes. For a moment, her face relaxed into a smile. And then her shoulders slumped again, and she pushed the cookie away and turned back to the muffin pans.

"This is one of the best cookies I've ever had," I told her. "No wonder they're your favorite." It was true, even if I still liked my mom's better. Also, Ms. Davis says that sometimes people need to be reminded of what their strengths are. I carefully lifted the rest of the pistachio-oatmeal bars out of the pan with a spatula and arranged them on a tray.

But Aunt Becky's shoulders didn't get any less slumpy.

I put parchment paper on cookie sheets for one batch each of her boring old cookies and thought about what else I could do, and Aunt Becky mixed oatmeal-raisin batter in the Enormous Mixer of Danger, and Great-Uncle Timothy changed the coffee in the coffeepot, even though no one had been in to buy any of the old coffee.

And then the door opened, and the big jingle bell jangled, and a lady with bright orange hair and emerald-green sunglasses and fuchsia lipstick and about fifty pins on her jacket brought the mail in. She saw me and stopped. "Well, then, who's this?" She plopped the mail down on the counter.

Great-Uncle Timothy opened his mouth and turned a bit red, but no words came out. Aunt Becky didn't look away from the mixer. I'm not sure if she couldn't stop right then or couldn't hear anything above the noise.

"I'm Fiona," I told the lady. "I'm staying with my relatives this summer, so I'm helping out here."

The lady tipped her head and studied me. "Let's see. . . . Are you Sheila's daughter?"

I nodded and felt my stomach twist, waiting for her to ask why I was here instead of with my mom.

But she didn't. "Nice to meet you, Fiona." She grinned at me. "I'm Renee, the downtown postal carrier. I deliver the mail and let people know what's happening."

I studied her. Her uniform was plain old navy, but everything else she was wearing was a different bright color. She

even had on two different socks, one orange with lime polka dots, one yellow with turquoise stars. I couldn't tell how she was going to fit into this story.

She saw me looking and grinned. "I like to keep things interesting."

"Then you should try one of these," I said, and handed her a cookie. "Aunt Becky says we can't sell them, so it's free."

Renee started to shake her head. Then she stopped and sniffed as the freshly baked cookie smell hit her nose. "Is this what smells so good?"

"It's a pistachio-oatmeal bar with raspberry jam. From a secret recipe," I told her. "We might never make them again."

She took a bite. She chewed slowly, staring at me. "Where did you learn to bake like this?"

"It isn't my recipe," I told her. "It's Aunt Becky's."

Renee straightened up. "Becky Jean Starke, you'd better make as many of these as you can, right now, because I'm going to tell the whole town about them."

Aunt Becky stared at Renee like she'd just turned into a dragon.

Actually, Renee would make a pretty good dragon. They like shiny, colorful things, too. And they're not at all shy.

"But my mother—" Aunt Becky began.

Renee frowned at her. "Don't give me that nonsense. You'd better stop worrying and start baking. And no more handing them out for free, either. Do you want to pay your bills or not?"

I decided I liked Renee. "Thank you," I told her. "I'm glad you like Aunt Becky's cookies."

"And I'm glad you're here," Renee replied, smiling. She finished her cookie, wiped a big smear of lipstick onto her napkin, and marched out the door, jingle bell clanging.

Now that's more like it, I thought.

Great-Uncle Timothy was still smiling, even if he did look kind of dazed.

Aunt Becky wasn't. I watched as she set the Enormous Mixer of Danger bowl aside, next to the cookie sheets that were waiting. She bent down and got another huge bowl out of a cupboard, fitting it onto the mixer. Then she picked up her special cookie recipe and read it through. As she measured oats and pistachios and dumped them into the bowl, I grinned. When dragons appear, things have to change. Apparently, even Aunt Becky knew that.

I found another pan for her special cookies and got it ready for her. Great-Uncle Timothy wandered over to the sink and started washing more dishes. Aunt Becky watched the mixer bowl like it was a crystal ball. No one else had come in.

Well, if they were good for now, I had other things I needed to do today. "Where's the library?" I asked. It was time to send some emails and do some research.

IT TURNED OUT THE LIBRARY WAS RIGHT DOWN THE STREET. THE TALL white guy at the desk helped me fill out the form to get a library card for the summer and said it was no problem when I told him I needed to go back to the bakery to get it signed.

He looked at me thoughtfully. "Are those new cookies as good as Renee said?"

Huh. Dragons move fast. "Yeah," I told him. "Want me to bring you one?" I didn't see anyone else there to help him, and I know librarians can't just close the library every time they want a cookie.

His face lit up. "Would you?" He pulled out his wallet and handed me a five-dollar bill. "Tell Becky that . . . um . . . Kevin says hi," he said hesitantly.

"Be right back," I told him.

Great-Uncle Timothy was at the bakery counter, selling the cookies I'd made to a line of people. They all stared at me as I ducked behind the counter. But then the lady buying a cookie turned and took a bite, and everyone watched her instead. She concentrated while she chewed, and then she smiled, and everyone's eyes followed her as she got back in line again. Aunt Becky was busy in the kitchen, spreading jam on the next batch of cookie dough.

I picked up a pen and put my form on the counter. "I need this signed to get my library card," I told Great-Uncle Timothy. "And Kevin at the library wants to buy a cookie. He says hi, Aunt Becky."

Aunt Becky froze for a minute. Like maybe she wasn't sure how to do basic friend stuff anymore.

"Do you want me to tell him hi back?" I asked. Fairy god-people have to be patient with people who are working stuff out. Even if it's really obvious stuff they should know.

Slowly, Aunt Becky nodded.

Great-Uncle Timothy didn't make me wait in line. He rang me up while a lady was looking in her purse for her glasses and gave me Kevin's change and a cookie in a little paper bag. He looked at the library-card form and hesitated for a minute, like he wasn't sure if he was authorized to decide whether I should get my own library card.

"You don't have to worry—I know how to keep track of my books and be a good library user," I explained. He'd only just met me, after all. "Just sign it, and then you can get back to helping people."

He looked at the long line of people, sighed, and signed it.

"Thanks," I said, and headed back to the library.

I gave Kevin his change and his cookie and my form, and told him that Aunt Becky said hi back. He said thanks and gave me my library card and a copy of the library's rules.

With that out of the way, I decided it was time to get some real work done. "I need to check my email, and I need to know how to get cookies like that out of a big pan without the first one breaking," I said. "Can you help me? And do you have any books about how to become a spy if you're an old lady? Or about fairy godpeople or baking magic? Or how to break curses? Oh, and do you have any of the Hamster Princess books?" Those books are my favorites, even though the fairy godpeople—er, the fairy godmice and godrats—were totally incompetent. They're funny, and they don't pretend that life's not hard work, even in fairy tales. I feel better every time I read one, no matter how many times I've read it before. And even though things were going pretty well so far, it seemed like a good idea to have one ready, just in case.

"Anything for the brave knight who brought me a cookie from the Forbidden Bakery," Kevin said, grinning at me.

I rolled my eyes. "Why would I want to be a knight? People shouldn't charge in waving swords before they even ask people what's up. It's not helpful."

He looked surprised. "I never really thought about it like that."

"Well, you should. And why did you call it the 'Forbidden Bakery'?" I asked.

His smile slipped. "Ask your aunt," he said. "Now let me show you how to get on the computer."

Dear Mom,

I found the library, so I can email you, like you asked. I hope you can email me, too. But I know you need to concentrate on what you need to learn there, not on emailing me all the time. If you can't, or you forget, it's okay.

Today I helped Aunt Becky make cookies and finally earn some money. I am fine. You don't need to worry about me. Just learn fast, so we can go home soon.

Love,
Fiona

P.S. I miss you.

Dear Ms. Davis,

Things are okay here. I am fine.

I already did my assignment. It wasn't hard at all to find someone who seemed unhappy. I decided to start with Aunt Becky. She's been making boring muffins and cookies for practically her whole life, because Great-Aunt Alta said she had to keep doing the same thing that wasn't working anyway. Like that's going to make anything better.

So I asked her what her favorite kind of cookie was. Have you ever heard of pistachio-oatmeal bars with raspberry jam? I asked her if I could make them. I thought maybe they'd make her feel better. She said yes, and I made them! They're pretty great. Then Renee the postal carrier told everybody in town about them, and the bakery finally got some customers. Okay, fine, maybe that part was me and Renee helping more than it was Aunt Becky helping herself. But it was Aunt Becky's recipe. And now she's making the cookies by herself. Does that count?

Anyway, Aunt Becky is off to a good start. I think it might be harder to help Great-Uncle Timothy, because he almost never talks. And Great-Aunt Alta says her problem is all the suffering in the world. So that might take me a while.

Your apprentice-fairy-godperson-in-training,
Fiona

P.S. What do you think it says about Aunt Becky that her favorite cookie is pistachio-oatmeal bars with raspberry jam?

4

BY THE TIME I finished sending my emails, Kevin had a whole stack of books for me to look at.

I said no to some cookbooks that just had the word "magic" in the title but didn't have any actual magic at all. He had the second Hamster Princess book, so I took that one to read again. And he found me a picture book about a girl who goes to stay with her grumpy uncle who's a baker and makes a huge garden on his roof. It didn't have real magic, and it isn't my uncle who's grumpy, but the pictures were pretty neat, so I checked it out. I also took a book about a girl who bakes magic cakes and a book about a boy who solves problems and helps a lady have her true dream bakery, even though that one wasn't actually magic, either.

Kevin's going to keep his eyes open for any more I might like.

He even printed some articles for me for free because I'm

a student. There were a couple about applying for spy jobs and one about how to hang the baking parchment over the side of your pan so you can lift your cookies out carefully and not break them. He said to tell Aunt Becky her cookies are amazing.

I told him thanks and hauled everything back to the bakery.

The glass case next to the cash register was full of plates of blueberry muffins, chocolate cupcakes with yellow sprinkles, and white cupcakes with pink sprinkles now. But no one was paying any attention to them. Every customer Great-Uncle Timothy helped wanted those cookies Renee had told them about.

Aunt Becky was plopping chocolate-chip-cookie dough onto the cookie sheet I'd greased for her. But I could smell more pistachio-oatmeal bars baking.

I washed my hands, put my apron and shower cap and gloves back on, got more jam and pistachios and oats out of the cupboard, and got more pans ready, the way the article said to do it.

At noon, after my stomach growled for the third time, I found some bread in one of the tall cupboards and made us all peanut butter and banana sandwiches. Aunt Becky took a five-minute break and slammed hers down, then washed her hands, put her gloves on, and went right back to baking. But I was getting to know her better, and I decided she looked kind of happy, in her own way.

We baked until two o'clock, when we ran out of raspberry jam.

I glanced at the sign on the door. The bakery was open until three o'clock. But the cookies wouldn't last until then. Well, not the good cookies anyway. The glass cases were still full of chocolate chip cookies and oatmeal-raisin cookies. Aunt Becky had baked every single thing on the menu in between batches of her special cookies. The bakery was hot, and the frosting on the cupcakes looked a little melty.

Aunt Becky slid the last pan of pistachio-oatmeal bars into the oven.

I looked at the customers that were still waiting. "What do we do?"

"Tell the people in line that they're the last," Aunt Becky told me. "Then put a note on the door that says there will be more pistachio-oatmeal bars with raspberry jam tomorrow." She was standing straight and tall, like she could handle anything.

So I did what she said. One guy said he wanted two dozen cookies, and I told him no, we didn't have that many left and that the people behind him deserved to try them, too. But we had plenty of chocolate chip cookies, if he wanted some of those.

He didn't.

"If you'd like to place a special order for tomorrow, we can have them ready first thing," Aunt Becky called from the kitchen, and the guy stopped grumbling and filled out the order form that Great-Uncle Timothy handed him.

When the last person left, clutching his cookie, I looked at the clock. Fifteen minutes until the bakery closed.

"Is that how your days usually go?" I asked.

Great-Uncle Timothy shook his head.

No one came in for the last fifteen minutes.

"So, what shall we make tomorrow?" I asked.

Aunt Becky opened up her secret recipe box.

But Great-Uncle Timothy spoke up, loud enough for Aunt Becky to hear, too. "Banana bread with chocolate chips." He got the same funny smile on his face that he'd had when Renee the postal carrier came in.

"Okay," I agreed.

"And blueberry bran muffins," Aunt Becky said, pulling out another card. "With ginger." She checked the cupboards and started a shopping list.

"Are you done making boring stuff now?" I asked. "Why don't you try some more experiments? Maybe you could make bread or something."

"Not unless you want to get up at four in the morning," Aunt Becky said. "It takes too long. We make muffins and cookies and—"

"Yeah, I got it," I told her. She didn't answer my other question. But since she'd already agreed to try some new things, I let it slide—for now. Change isn't that easy, after all.

Great-Uncle Timothy went to the store while Aunt Becky and I packed up all the boring stuff that hadn't sold into boxes, which we'd drop off at the food bank on our way home. I wondered if that was what they'd been doing every day for who knows how long: baking stuff, waiting for someone to buy it, then giving it all away. I was glad it wouldn't go to waste. But I was also glad she'd finally decided to make something that people wanted to buy.

Aunt Becky washed the dishes, and I put away the ones

that had dried. When we'd finished, I told her I thought I'd better learn how to use the cash register, in case of an emergency, like if Great-Uncle Timothy needed to use the bathroom while she was busy operating the Enormous Mixer of Danger.

Aunt Becky thought about that for a minute. Then she nodded and showed me how. It's not too bad. Mostly, you just have to concentrate on putting the price in correctly and counting back the change the right way. You have to go slowly and carefully and not let anyone rush or distract you while you're doing the money part.

I decided we'd better get our real talk done before Great-Uncle Timothy came back. "I know you didn't think this was going to be a good idea," I told her. "But thanks for letting me make the cookies anyway. I hope you're glad you did now."

Aunt Becky didn't say anything. But she didn't really need to. She smiled a real smile again, and that told me everything I needed to know.

THAT NIGHT AFTER DINNER, I MADE A THANK-YOU CARD FOR RENEE THE postal carrier with my construction paper and glue stick and stickers and markers. I made a paper cutout of a dragon for the cover and wrote "Thank you for telling everyone about our cookies!" inside. Then I cleaned up all the little bits of leftover cut paper by sticking them all over the card, inside and out, kind of like confetti. When the glue was dry, I took it down for Aunt Becky and Great-Uncle Timothy to sign.

Aunt Becky just signed her name. I thought she should at least write her own note or something. But I decided not to push it.

Great-Uncle Timothy examined the card carefully, even the back. Then he picked one of the little paper bits I'd glued inside and drew a tiny picture around it, so it turned into a raccoon holding one of Aunt Becky's cookies. Even its fur looked furry. He signed his name next to it.

"That's beautiful!" I said. "Where did you learn to draw like that? Do you decorate cakes? If you don't, why do you have a bakery? Why not just be an artist?"

He just shrugged. He closed the card and handed it back to me.

"Do you think Great-Aunt Alta wants to sign it, too?" I asked.

Very slowly, he shook his head no. I didn't really think so, either. And just like that, all my good feelings turned into dust and swirled away, until I was stuck staring at a huge black lake of sadness, with no magic boat. I missed my mom. I did not want to be here anymore.

I sighed and went to read one of my library books.

THE NEXT MORNING WASN'T EASIER. BUT I TOOK A DEEP BREATH, GOT myself up, and got ready. The card I made was right where

I left it. I opened it up and looked at the tiny raccoon again, until I felt like I could leave my room. Cards don't deliver themselves, after all. And no one else here was fixing anything.

So I went down to the kitchen and I gave Great-Aunt Alta the articles about how to apply for spy jobs. "Just in case," I told her.

She acted like she had no idea what I was talking about. Maybe she was practicing her spy work. But she handed me the jam jar along with the yogurt container. Progress! "Another day begins: sour, mixed with sweet," she intoned, like she was doing a depressing version of the Pledge of Allegiance. "It will not last."

"That's all right," I said, handing them back. "Aunt Becky and I are going to make blueberry bran muffins with ginger today, and I want to try one." I figured I'd better try our banana bread with chocolate chips, too, but chocolate chips aren't for breakfast.

I guess I forgot that she didn't know about our plans yet. Instead of asking sensible questions, she gave me a real-life example of why my other relatives don't tell her anything.

"What madness is this?" she cried. "What reason do you have to change the way things have always been done—to change the very lifeblood of the Starke Brothers Bakery?" She stepped back with her hand pressed up above her boobs like someone in a play.

Actually, her voice kind of sounded like she could be in a play, too. I don't think she thought she was yelling, but school rules say if someone can hear you all the way across the gym, that's yelling.

"What are you talking about?" I asked. "No one puts blood in muffins. That's just gross."

Great-Aunt Alta didn't explain herself. She just got louder. Her words rolled out so loud that nobody could think above all the noise. "Never could I have imagined that a daughter of mine could strike at her family's pride and joy in such a way!"

Aunt Becky's eyes were wide and unhappy. "Mother—"

But Great-Aunt Alta wasn't about to let anyone else talk. "Generations of Starkes, abandoned and forgotten!" she thundered on. "My father's recipe, lost! My brother's memory, forsaken!"

"I'm going to go get ready," I said in the sudden silence. "You should, too, Aunt Becky, or we'll be late." I ran upstairs to my room without looking back.

When I got there, I sat down on the bed and clutched my stomach so it wouldn't wobble so much. My heart was pounding. I don't like it when people yell and get upset. That's when things get out of control. It makes me feel like my blood's been turned to lava, flowing through my body and making me shake. It makes me want to run.

But this was not my first volcano. Ms. Davis and I made a

plan for when this happens. So I took a deep breath, got out my pen and my notebook, and answered the questions we thought up for times like this.

1. Do I feel like someone might get hurt?

No, I decided. Great-Aunt Alta was mad at Aunt Becky, not me, and she wasn't acting like she was going to do anything to anyone. She was in control of her body, not crashing into things or falling down. She was just mad, and loud. I felt my lava-blood cool down a little bit, and I pictured some of that extra energy radiating off me and into the air around me, like the heaters in our apartment building back home.

2. Will things get better faster if I call an adult I trust?

This one took some thought. Ms. Davis could help me, of course. So could the friend she'd asked to help me if I needed it while I was here. I hadn't met Mr. Rivera yet, but Ms. Davis had given me his phone number and told me I could call him anytime, just like I call her.

But Great-Aunt Alta's voice had faded away, and it was time to leave for the bakery. I was meeting Mr. Rivera at the library later today anyway. So I decided to wait—we could talk about it then.

I wrote "No." My lava-blood got bored waiting around, and cooled down some more. I took another deep breath and thought about how when lava cools down, it makes gray rocks that look kind of wrinkly, and how lizards like to sleep on them. (I did a report on lava once.)

3. Is my brain giving me extra energy that helps me? Or extra energy that gets in my way?

If you have to do something that takes a lot of energy, like run away or yell for help or maybe even lift a car off some kid who's stuck underneath, you might need that extra energy. But all I had to do was tell Great-Aunt Alta how I felt, and I didn't even have to do that right now.

Extra energy that gets in my way, I decided, and the last of the lava drained out of my blood.

I took a deep breath. Then I closed my notebook, put it in my backpack with the library books I was done with, and went back downstairs.

WE WERE ALL QUIET ON THE WAY TO THE BAKERY. BUT THEN IT WAS time to get back to my fairy-godperson duties. "I'm sorry your mom yelled at you," I told Aunt Becky. "But baking new muffins is not something she should yell about. You know that, right? So what's up with that?"

Aunt Becky was quiet while she unlocked the door and got her apron and gloves and everything on. I didn't rush her. But I didn't stop waiting for an answer, either.

Finally, she sighed. "Right before Uncle Robert died, he and my mother had a huge argument. A bad one. She said she'd never speak to him again. He left, and got into a car accident, and . . . she never did."

"What were they fighting about?" I asked. I wasn't exactly surprised to learn that my granddad hadn't always gotten along with Great-Aunt Alta.

"He was moving away, and leaving the bakery," Aunt Becky said, looking tired. "Renee told me. Mother still doesn't talk about it. He wanted to go back to school, maybe do something with engineering. They were going to move closer to his wife's family, so they could help out while your mother was little."

I nodded. I knew that Mom's grandparents had helped out when she was little, especially after her dad died, just like my grandmom helped Mom take care of me. If she was still alive, I'd be staying with her this summer.

Aunt Becky stared out the bakery window like she could see into the past. "I don't know what my mother was like before then. But after . . . Well, now she needs everything to be just the way it was, frozen in time. Like, if things stay that way, maybe he'll come back."

"That's not how things work, though," I pointed out. "Not even in stories. Maybe she wishes they did, but they don't."

Aunt Becky didn't say anything. She didn't look so good. Probably she didn't like yelling, either.

I kept going. "We promised people we'd make more of your favorite cookies today, and we took that guy's special order. You don't have to, if it's too scary. We could call him and tell him that we're sorry, we can't do it after all." I waited a moment. "But then what? Are you only going to bake boring stuff from now on? Or are you going to try something new, like you wanted to?"

Aunt Becky walked over to the recipes taped up on the wall above the back counter. They were the ones she'd been making for years and years and years: blueberry muffins, chocolate chip cookies, oatmeal-raisin cookies, chocolate cupcakes with yellow sprinkles, white cupcakes with pink sprinkles, and banana bread (without any chocolate chips).

Then she straightened up and turned back to me. "I'll start on the pistachio-oatmeal bars. You can find the muffin recipe in my box."

I smiled and got to work.

Aunt Becky's secret recipe box wasn't very big, but it was packed with little cards, each with a handwritten recipe. There wasn't a table of contents or an index or anything. They weren't even alphabetical. And some of them were hard to read and had things crossed out and changed and added, like she'd been testing them out. Some of them looked a little too weird for me or just not my style. (Who wants to eat chocolate chip cookies with garlic?) But none of them were boring.

"You know how to make pizza?" I said. "Can we make it sometime?"

Aunt Becky nodded. "I used to make it all the time with— with a friend of mine."

I pulled out the blueberry-bran-muffin card and held it up. "Want me to get the muffin ingredients out for you?"

"That would be great," she said, and gave me another real smile. She finished shaking the topping on the pans of pistachio-oatmeal bars and slid them into the first two ovens.

So I got all the ingredients out for the new muffins and one of the big muffin pans. "What color should these muffin papers be?" I asked.

Aunt Becky put her hands on her hips and looked me straight in the eye. "Blue."

I grinned. Aunt Becky had joined the rebel ranks at last.

5

THERE WERE STACKS and stacks of blue papers in the cupboard. I filled the muffin pan with them while Aunt Becky measured and mixed. After she scooped the batter into each cup, she handed a container of crystallized ginger to Great-Uncle Timothy. He smiled and put a sugar-covered chunk on top of each scoop of muffin batter.

The timer went off. Aunt Becky pulled the pistachio-oatmeal bars out of the first two ovens and slid the muffins into the third. She moved on to the chocolate cupcakes while we waited for the pistachio-oatmeal bars to cool.

When they were finally ready, Aunt Becky grabbed hold of the baking parchment that was hanging over the edges of the first pan, and lifted the whole big slab of cookies out of the pan and onto the counter. She didn't drop it, and none of them broke. She cut the slab up into perfect little cookies, without a single broken one.

"Go, Team Pistachio-Oatmeal Bar!" I said, and held up my hand for a high five.

Aunt Becky looked at my hand like she was really not sure what she was supposed to do with it.

"High five!" I explained. It was a little awkward, hanging out with my hand still up. But I knew she wasn't doing it to be mean. It was kind of sad she didn't know what to do with a high five when one came her way. A good fairy godperson wouldn't let her continue like that without helping. "You know what a high five is, right?"

She nodded slowly and carefully smacked my hand with hers. Then she smiled, another real smile. "High five," she said quietly.

We were going to have to work on her enthusiasm. But at least she was trying.

"So, how did you get this muffin recipe?" I asked. The blueberries and ginger were warming up in the oven now, beating out the smell of warm raspberry jam and coffee.

She folded her arms and stared at the bakery cases, but not like she was really seeing them. "Every time I bake the same old blueberry muffins, I think: What if I changed something?"

"Sure. Why wouldn't you? I would have gotten bored the first week."

She sighed. "It was never the right time to make a fuss about it. But sometimes I come up with a new twist. Something that tastes so delicious in my mind, I can't let it go. So I write it down." She waved a hand at the secret recipe box.

"You can taste things in your head?" I asked. "Is that your superpower or something?"

She grinned. "Can't you imagine what those muffins will taste like? You haven't tried them, but you can smell them, right?"

I sniffed again and thought about it. "I guess."

"Well, I practiced. I can remember what things taste like, and I combine them in my imagination and see what I think." She took a deep breath, like she had to confess something. "I did research, too, some days. After the cases were full, Uncle Timothy watched the bakery and I went to the library."

I waited, but she didn't say anything else, just looked at me. "Sure," I said. "I go to the library all the time. How else are you supposed to learn anything when you aren't in school?"

"Exactly!" she said, quiet but triumphant. "I don't go anywhere—I don't do anything—but I read everything. Everything!" She was pacing around the kitchen now, smacking her fist into her palm like a woman on a mission. "I read what people in other countries cook, what chefs in city restaurants cook—what people have tried and what other people think. It all goes in here." She tapped her forehead. "Once in a while, I sneak a change into a recipe. My mother has no idea I use butter instead of shortening in our cupcakes! But even when I can't try it, I remember. I research the kinds of changes people make—all the possibilities—and I write it down."

"Good job," I told her. I wasn't sure what the big deal was. But fairy godpeople are supposed to be encouraging.

"I'm not the first person to put blueberries in bran muffins, so I made notes on how other bakers did theirs. Same with adding ginger. And then I put all those notes together, and I came up with my own version."

"I never thought of doing that," I said. "But I guess if everyone else's worked, these probably will, too."

Aunt Becky grinned. "They won't just work—they'll be amazing."

The timer over the muffin oven dinged and stopped ticking. Even Great-Uncle Timothy came over to watch as Aunt Becky opened the oven door. She pulled out the pans and set them on the counter to cool.

They did smell awfully good. And they looked good, too—dark brown from the bran, with blueberries like little meteors in craters all over. Somehow Aunt Becky had made it so they didn't all sink to the bottom. The ginger on top sparkled like crystals, hinting at the ground ginger she'd mixed inside.

My stomach grumbled, and Aunt Becky laughed. "Five minutes," she said, shaking her finger at it, like a pretend teacher. But I could tell she was happy my stomach wanted to eat what she made.

Which reminded me. "Can we do the banana bread with chocolate chips next?"

"Sure," Aunt Becky said.

She almost looked and sounded like a normal person now. Maybe this would all be a lot easier than I'd thought. Even Great-Uncle Timothy smiled a tiny smile.

Five minutes later, Aunt Becky brought us each a muffin. I peeled the paper off carefully, so the blueberries wouldn't stick to it and get pulled out. Then I took a bite.

It really was amazing. Kind of toasty somehow. The ginger didn't taste like gingerbread, but like something warm inside you that you didn't know was there. Like happiness, or love. It didn't get in the way of the sweetness of the blueberries, either. It just made everything a little bit better.

"Okay, you were right," I told her. "Good thing you made an enormous batch."

She grinned.

Great-Uncle Timothy was standing there with his eyes closed, eating his muffin. He had a dreamy smile on his face. I wondered what he was wishing for.

But it seemed like he didn't have an easy time answering questions, and I know that's a tough one to answer when you don't know people very well. So I let him be. For now.

THE BAKERY DOOR RATTLED, JANGLING THE BELL. I LOOKED UP. RENEE and the guy who'd placed the special order for cookies were waiting outside. The guy tapped his watch and frowned when he saw me looking.

Great-Uncle Timothy's eyes snapped open. He set down his muffin and hurried over to the coffeepot.

It was time to open.

"Can you unlock the door and flip the sign around?" Aunt Becky asked me.

Renee grinned at me through the glass as I unlocked it.

"Welcome to Starke Brothers Bakery," I announced, holding the door open. "Today's specials include blueberry bran muffins with ginger—you really should try one, Renee—and banana bread with chocolate chips . . . when it's ready."

The guy didn't listen to me. He barged in and headed straight to the register. "I'm picking up a special order," he told Great-Uncle Timothy, already impatient, even though he'd just gotten here.

But Great-Uncle Timothy didn't freeze or get freaked out. He nodded slowly, then pushed the box of cookies Aunt Becky had packed up across the counter and punched the numbers into the register at his usual speed.

Renee rolled her eyes as the guy rushed off. "Some people and their manners—or lack thereof," she said, handing me the mail. "Now, what's this about muffins? Is that what I'm smelling?"

"Probably," I told her. "The toasty smell is the muffins."

Renee took a long sniff. "Well, it all smells delicious," she said.

I set the mail down and gave her the card we'd made for her. She opened it, and froze for a second. Then she looked at Great-Uncle Timothy's back for a long time, while he did something to the coffee machine. "Thank you," she said slowly.

"I'm not sure he wants to talk about his art just yet," I said very quietly. "It might be private, or he might just not really talk all that much."

Renee tipped her head and looked at me. "I like you, Fiona."

I grinned at her. "I like you, too." And then, because I trusted her to understand that it was a good thing, I told her, "The dragon reminded me of you."

She examined the dragon on the front of the card. I'd cut the points off a glittery star sticker to give her sparkling claws, and she had a hoard of stars and flowers and hearts. "It's perfect," she said. "Now, I can't delay my mail route, not even for banana bread, so I'll have to try that when I stop by tomorrow. But I need one of those muffins."

Great-Uncle Timothy didn't look at her as he put her muffin in a bag and rang her up and gave her her change. But Renee didn't seem to mind. Instead, she just talked and talked, telling me all about what everyone had said about Aunt Becky's cookies.

Aunt Becky didn't say anything. But I could tell she was listening to every word, standing tall and proud as she mixed up the banana bread in the Enormous Mixer of Danger.

After Renee left, I reminded Aunt Becky and Great-Uncle Timothy that I had to go to the library to meet Ms. Davis's friend Mr. Rivera. "Are you going to be okay without me?" The line wasn't as long as yesterday, but people kept coming in.

Great-Uncle Timothy nodded.

"Can I take one of your special muffins for him?" I asked. I knew they had to feed me, but that didn't mean I could give all the bakery food away to anyone I met without asking. Not when they were making it to sell.

"Go ahead," Aunt Becky told me. So I put a muffin and a napkin in a bag to take to Mr. Rivera. I knew I should be glad he'd agreed to help me. *But he isn't Ms. Davis,* I thought as I left the bakery and walked slowly down the sidewalk to the library. I didn't want to talk to some stranger about my private feelings, even if Ms. Davis thought it was a good idea.

I gave myself a little shake and picked up my pace. Waiting and worrying about something that might happen was princess thinking, I reminded myself. I didn't need any of that.

I guess I wasn't really watching where I was going, because I bumped into something and knocked it over. I stopped and set it upright again.

Then I realized what my eyes were staring at: one of those chalkboard signs that's folded in half at the top, standing on the sidewalk so it would catch people's attention. It was in front of a barbershop, and it said WEEKLY SPECIAL: BUZZ

CUT—$10. Someone had drawn a picture of what I guess was supposed to be a guy's head. Too bad they didn't know any good artists . . . like Great-Uncle Timothy.

KEVIN WAS AT THE DESK AT THE LIBRARY AGAIN. HE GRINNED AT ME when I came in the door. "What's Becky baking today?" he asked. "More cookies?"

"Yeah, more of those, plus blueberry bran muffins with ginger, and banana bread with chocolate chips. I can go get you something after I'm done here, if you want. But I have to talk to Mr. Rivera first."

He grinned. "Right! Ernesto's in the meeting room. It's a little quieter in there."

I looked through the glass door where he pointed, and saw a guy with black hair and medium brown skin sitting at a long table. He smiled and waved.

I swallowed hard. *I can do this,* I reminded myself. I breathed in and held it. Then I breathed it all back out.

"I've got one of the other Hamster Princess books for you," Kevin said. "I saw it come back in and thought you might want it."

I nodded, and he checked it out and handed it to me. "Thanks," I told him. *I can do this.* And then, if I needed a break, I could escape into a great book for a while.

I marched over to the meeting room and opened the door. Before I could lose my nerve, I handed the bag to Mr.

Rivera. "I'm Fiona," I told him. "My aunt made these amazing muffins."

"Nice to meet you, Fiona. I'm Ernesto Rivera." He grinned at me—definitely a real smile, not one of those poor-you, whatever-you-say-dear smiles. He opened the bag and took a long sniff. "Becky made this?" he asked. "I thought she only made regular blueberry muffins."

"Not anymore!" I said triumphantly, sitting down across

from him. Then I told him the story of Aunt Becky's pistachio-oatmeal bars.

"Nice! I'm glad she's finally baking what she wants to." He peeled back the paper and took a bite of his muffin. His eyebrows went up as he chewed. "Make that really, *really* glad," he said once his mouth wasn't full.

"How do you know her?" I asked.

"It's a small town," he said. "You should ask her about the time she and her friend Annie made a cake for the town festival's baking competition. It had so much frosting, it took four people to lift it!" He shook his head, grinning.

"If she used to be fun, how did she get so quiet and sad?" I asked. "If she had friends, why didn't they help her?"

Mr. Rivera sighed, his smile fading. "People make their own choices. Sometimes it's hard to help. No matter how much we want to, we can't help people until they're ready to help themselves."

That's what Ms. Davis always says, too. But that's not how fairy tales work, so I know better.

"Sure, for regular people," I told him. "But I'm training to be a fairy godperson. Fairy godpeople can always help, no matter how bad things are. Even when someone's stuck in a dungeon or banished from their kingdom or whatever. Even when they're cursed. I've been practicing on Aunt Becky—and look what I've done already!"

"Ms. Davis mentioned your lessons," he said, nodding. "What are you working on now?"

So I told him all about the first lesson. "Now I need to do something small to help Great-Uncle Timothy, and then maybe Great-Aunt Alta," I told him. "She's the hardest. But I'll think of something."

"You mean, find something that they can do to help themselves—right?" Mr. Rivera studied my face. "Sounds like they're in good hands. Now, then—what about you? Is there anything you want to talk about? Or anything I can help you out with?"

"Not really," I said. "I'm fine."

He waited for me to say something, still smiling, just like Ms. Davis always does.

I sighed, and thought about it some more. "I'm not moping around or anything," I said at last. "Not like Aunt Becky was. I mean, I miss my mom, and I'm still not happy about being here for the summer—no offense."

"None taken," he said calmly. "I bet this wasn't an easy change for you."

I nodded. "But I have food to eat, and the electricity works, and I got my library card, so I can check my email. I need a bus pass and a route map, though, in case someone forgets to pick me up or is too busy when I want to go somewhere. The bakery is interesting, but I don't want to spend my whole summer there. And I'm not getting stuck in the house with Great-Aunt Alta being all gloomy and doomy."

He rubbed at his chin thoughtfully. "I could help you get

a bus pass. But there aren't many buses here, and they don't run that often. Most kids ride their bikes instead. Do you know how to ride one?"

"Sure," I said. "But I didn't bring mine." I hadn't thought about that. Nobody told me I'd need it here. I felt my chest get tighter and my blood start to heat up. How can I be prepared when I don't know what will happen?

Mr. Rivera nodded, slow and calm. "I've got a niece who just started driving," he said. "I'll check with her and see if you could borrow her old bike for the summer. What do you think?"

I took a breath before I answered. "Okay. But if I ride someone else's bike, I have to wear a helmet that fits. I promised Ms. Davis."

"I bet we have a helmet around you could borrow. Anything else you want to talk about?"

I thought about Great-Aunt Alta yelling at Aunt Becky. But I didn't really want to talk about that in our first conversation. Besides, I hadn't tried the things I knew how to try yet. "Nah, I'm fine," I said. "Are we done?"

MR. RIVERA STAYED IN THE MEETING ROOM SO HE COULD FINISH EATing his muffin without getting crumbs all over the library.

I decided to check my email and do more research. As I walked by the kids' section, a girl looked up from her book.

She was small, but she didn't look much younger than me. She had dark brown skin and really curly black hair and tiny gold earrings. "Are you a good witch or a bad witch?" she asked me.

"I'm not a witch at all!" I said automatically. "How about you?"

"A good witch," she said. "Usually. I'm Julia."

"I'm Fiona," I said. "Don't you think Glinda is actually more of a fairy godmother, though? I mean, she pretty much just helps Dorothy get her wish, right? And she helps her with her princess problems—getting lost far from home, and falling asleep while she has stuff she's supposed to be doing, and not knowing how to use her gear properly."

"Nah, she's a witch," Julia said firmly. "You just don't see everything she's doing be-cause the movie is from Dorothy's point of view."

Hmm. "You don't think that good-witch, bad-witch thing is that simple, though, do you?"

"Of course not," she said. "You can't tell what kind of person someone is by what color hat they wear or what they look like. That's just wrong. And every story is from *someone's* point of view. Just because they think something doesn't mean it's true for everyone."

"Fairy tales aren't like that," I said. "They're about the whole story—you don't just see them through one person's eyes."

"Yeah, you do." She folded her arms. "You might not hear everything Cinderella's thinking, but it's still all about her, not her stepsisters. They had stories, too—we just don't know them."

"I guess," I said slowly, thinking hard. "Is that why they only tell us about the fairy godmothers when they're helping the princess whose story it is?"

"Sure," Julia said. "Maybe that fairy godmother's real goal was to thwart one of the stepsisters who'd wronged her and keep her from getting her dream guy, and she only helped Cinderella because of that. We just don't know, because Cinderella thinks it's all about her." She grinned. "What kinds of books do you like?"

I shrugged. "Funny books with magic, usually."

Her face lit up. "Me too! I'm going to find you some books."

"Okay, but I have to go check my email," I told her.

Dearest Fiona,

I love you so much, brave girl. I'm doing everything they say so we can be back home before you know it. Just between you and me, I don't think it will take long at all. I might not even need to be here, not really. Not like some of the people here.

   I miss you so much. Stay strong for me.

Love,
Mom

Dear Mom,

I love you, too. I know you can do this. I miss you, too.
   I'm ready to go home as soon as you are.

Love,
Fiona

I'd promised Ms. Davis I wouldn't keep reminding Mom that I could come home and help her. So, even though I wanted to, I didn't.

Dear Fiona,

Nice work so far on your first lesson! Those cookies sound delicious. Sometimes it's hard to stand back and let people help themselves. Especially when they don't seem all that good at it yet. But that just means they need more practice, right? I'm sure you'll find a way to help your aunt help herself, too.

Tell me more about how things are going with you. Do you have what you need there? What do you think of Mr. Rivera? Have you found anything fun to do for yourself in your new town? Read any good books lately?

Sincerely,
Nia Davis

P.S. Don't forget to email your mom and tell her you love her. You know those words are always better out than in. Even—maybe especially—when we're dealing with some mixed-up feelings.

Dear Ms. Davis,

I am still fine. We forgot one thing when we made my packing list—my bike. (And my helmet.) Maybe it wouldn't have fit in the car. But Mr. Rivera is going to see if I can borrow a bike and a helmet from his niece. He seems fine so far.

I already told my mom. That I love her, not that I have mixed-up feelings. I don't want her to waste her time worrying about me. She says she can probably be done really soon. If that happens, will you still send me the rest of my lessons?

Your apprentice-fairy-godperson-in-training,
Fiona

P.S. Do you think that's something that will really happen? Or just something she wishes would happen? She gets confused about that sometimes.

P.P.S. A girl named Julia is finding some books she wants me to read, so I have to go now.

6

JUST LIKE MAGIC, Julia came up to my computer then, with a pile of books she could barely see over.

"Okay, tell me which of these you've read," she commanded.

I sorted them into two piles. "Read that. . . . I love that one! I might read it again. . . . I don't know that one."

She grinned. "It's *so good*! You have to read it."

"Okay," I told her. I hesitated for a minute. "But I need to know: Does anything really sad happen in it? Because I'm not up for that."

She didn't ask me why or tell me to get over it. She just thought hard, and then shook her head. "Not in that one. But don't read this one right now, if you don't want sad parts." She put the stack I wasn't taking on the cart for books to go back on the shelf.

Kevin had found a new book about baking for me. This one didn't have any actual magic, either. But it looked like something Aunt Becky might want for research—recipes with a little twist that she could probably imagine tasting.

So I checked it out, along with my stack from Julia. "Have you read this series?" I showed Julia the Hamster Princess book Kevin had saved for me.

"Those are so good!" she cried. "That reminds me—" She disappeared back into the kids' section.

Mr. Rivera came out of the meeting room. "Fiona, can I walk you back to the bakery? I think Julia should try your aunt's new muffins. I can give you a hand with all these books, if that's okay."

"Okay," I said, wondering how he knew Julia. She hadn't seemed like she needed any help.

Julia rushed back from the kids' section, clutching a book with a witch on the cover. "You have to read this, too—it's by the same author!" she said. She waved a hand at Mr. Rivera. "This is my dad."

"We met," I said, turning it over in my brain. Had Mr. Rivera told her she had to be nice to me?

She shoved the book at me again and rolled her eyes. "I mean, you don't *have* to read it, but why wouldn't you? It's *so good!*"

Julia didn't act like anyone was making her do anything. I took the book. "Thanks."

"Jules, I'm going to walk Fiona back to the bakery," Mr. Rivera said. "You want to come with us or stay here?"

"I'll come," Julia said.

"Will somebody bring me something?" Kevin asked plaintively as he checked out the book Julia had found for me.

"Sure," I told him. "Blueberry bran muffin with ginger or banana bread with chocolate chips? Or do you want another pistachio-oatmeal bar?"

"How about a muffin *and* a piece of banana bread," he told me, handing over some cash. "That way I can try everything."

WHILE WE WALKED, I TOLD JULIA ABOUT AUNT BECKY'S NEW COOKIES, and Renee telling everyone, and the card we made for her, and Great-Uncle Timothy's drawing. She seemed pretty interested.

When we got to the bakery, Great-Aunt Alta was there. I guess it was good to know she could leave the house. I'd been starting to wonder if a bad fairy or someone had trapped her there. But unfortunately she was yelling again.

"Never in all my days . . ." I could hear her voice thundering out as the door opened and people fled. They weren't carrying any bakery bags, either.

I looked around for Julia, but she'd vanished. My stomach twisted, and my blood filled up with lava again. People don't like it when your family is cursed and out of control. Maybe she didn't want to be friends anymore.

I took a deep breath and looked up at Mr. Rivera. "I'm

really sorry if Great-Aunt Alta scared Julia. I don't think she knows how she sounds to other people, or that they don't like it when she yells."

"I'll look out for Julia. I think she'll be okay," he told me thoughtfully. "But it sounds like you don't like yelling. Has Alta been yelling at you?"

"Not at me," I told him. "Just . . . around me, mostly at Aunt Becky. I don't like it, but I haven't asked her not to yet."

"Would you like me to ask her for you?" he said.

I thought about it. But I was the one who was supposed to be helping Aunt Becky. "Nah, I can do it." I took a deep breath and reminded my blood that lava didn't belong there, since I was not a volcano. "You can come, though, if you want."

He nodded and opened the door for me.

Great-Aunt Alta was standing in the middle of the bakery, still yelling. "To think that a daughter of mine . . ."

Julia was standing right in front of her. She didn't look scared at all. She looked interested. "Hey, lady, I'm trying to tell you something!" she bellowed.

Great-Aunt Alta looked down, shocked.

"I like your dress," Julia told her, smiling.

I wasn't surprised. It was another very witchy dress—long and black and kind of old-looking.

Before Great-Aunt Alta could react, Julia turned to Great-Uncle Timothy. "Can I have a muffin and two pieces of banana bread?" she asked. She looked back at us. "Hey, Dad, get over here—it's our turn."

Mr. Rivera went up to the counter and dug out his wallet, smiling at Great-Uncle Timothy. He nodded at Aunt Becky, who stood frozen by the mixer, her face pale. "Your new muffins are delicious."

Great-Aunt Alta took a deep breath.

But I pay attention, so I spoke up first. "You might not realize this, but I think you're scaring the customers," I told her. "People don't like it when you get so loud."

I saw Mr. Rivera watching me. He nodded and smiled.

"And I don't like it when people yell, either," I said. "It makes me uncomfortable. So, if there's something you want to talk to Aunt Becky about, could you please keep it down? And wait until she's not trying to work at the same time?"

Great-Aunt Alta's eyebrows flew up. "You don't understand . . ."

I waited for her to say what she wanted to say. If you tell
somebody something, it's fair to give them a chance to talk,
too. At least until they stop being reasonable about it.

But she just trailed off, like maybe even she wasn't sure
what she was saying anymore.

"Really, there's nothing to yell about," I told her, my
blood calming down a little now that it didn't feel like lightning was about to hit any of us. "Maybe you're scared about
the bakery not doing well, but there were lots of people here
when I left."

"These are amazing!" Julia said, taking a huge bite of
her muffin. She chewed, and grinned, and chewed some
more.

"Did you even try Aunt Becky's new recipes?" I asked
Great-Aunt Alta.

Her eyes narrowed. "Never!" Then she turned, like a
huge black bat, and stormed out of the bakery.

Mr. Rivera smiled at me. "Great work," he said softly.
"You doing all right?"

I nodded. "I should see how Aunt Becky's doing, though."

Julia went back up to Great-Uncle Timothy. "Fiona says
you can draw really well," she said. "Will you draw a witch
on my bag?"

Aunt Becky came around the counter and hurried over

to me. "I'm sorry you were here for that. Sometimes my mother . . ." She sighed. "I'm sorry," she said again.

"I'm sorry she yelled at you, too," I told her. "You don't have to take it, though. You can tell her you don't like it, that it makes you feel bad."

She hesitated, like she was trying to find the words to tell me why she couldn't—and then she nodded. "You're right," she said. "I could." She straightened up and looked at Mr. Rivera. "You look familiar."

He smiled. "Ernesto Rivera—we went to school together, but I was a couple years behind you. That's my daughter, Julia."

Aunt Becky's face went red. "Of course, Fiona mentioned you. My mother doesn't really mean . . ." She trailed off, glancing at me and then back at him. "I'll try harder."

"Thanks," he said. "I think Fiona will appreciate that." He handed me the rest of my library books, and I stacked them on the counter. "Fiona, I have to go back to the library. Want me to take something to Kevin?"

"Sure," I said. "Great-Uncle Timothy, Kevin wants a new muffin and a piece of new banana bread, please. Here's his money."

"Look what he drew for me!" Julia said, holding up her bakery bag.

It was Julia, tiny earrings and all, with a witch hat and a long black dress like Great-Aunt Alta's. The sky behind her was stormy, with clouds and a moon and a shadowy owl in a tree.

"That's amazing!" I said. "Thanks for doing that for my friend."

Then I realized what I'd said, and I got nervous. What if Julia wasn't actually my friend? We'd only just met.

But she just grinned and said, "Yeah, thanks!"

Great-Uncle Timothy smiled, too.

"We should hang out," Julia went on. "I want to hear what you think of those books." She ripped off a little piece of her bakery bag and wrote something on it. She handed it to me. "Call me, okay?"

I smiled. "Okay."

Maybe I wasn't wrong about having a friend.

7

AFTER MR. RIVERA and Julia left, the bakery was quiet. I thought I might as well get some answers before our customers figured out Great-Aunt Alta had left. "Why does Kevin at the library call this the 'Forbidden Bakery'?"

Aunt Becky sighed. "His sister didn't want him to come here. He used to stop by anyway, until I told him not to."

"Why?" I asked. "Don't you need customers? Do you hate his guts or something?"

She shook her head. "It was a long time ago. . . . I'm not even sure I understand why anymore. His sister, Annie, and I had a fight."

"With punching?" I asked. I couldn't really imagine Aunt Becky punching anyone, but who knew? "Or just an argument?"

"An argument . . . about frosting," she said, wrinkling her nose. "It sounds so stupid now—and it was! But some things get harder to fix the longer they last." She looked at me. "Take my advice: stop and think before you say something that you know will hurt someone else. Those mistakes will haunt you for the rest of your life." She stared out the window like she was thinking about all the suffering in the world.

Honestly, what was up with these people? "We all make mistakes," I told her. "We just have to learn from them, and do better next time. Did you ever apologize, if it doesn't even matter to you anymore? How long ago was this, anyway?"

"I was eighteen," Aunt Becky said softly. "Young and foolish."

I rolled my eyes. I'd thought Great-Aunt Alta had trapped Aunt Becky in a princess tower. Not a real one—one made out of sadness and really boring recipes. But it sounded like Aunt Becky had trapped herself there, with her own stubbornness and not wanting to apologize.

Whatever. Enough was enough. "So get over yourself, and tell her you're sorry you hurt her feelings."

"I can't," she said.

I folded my arms. I'd heard this kind of talk before. "Can't?" I asked. "Or won't?"

She stared at me, surprised.

"Come on—what's stopping you?" I asked. "Aren't you ready to be done with this?"

"She won't listen!" The words burst out of her. "I know her—I know she won't."

That sounded like another excuse to me. But it seemed important to Aunt Becky, so I stopped and thought before I said anything.

Aunt Becky wasn't used to using her words, I realized. Maybe they weren't what she was best at. Maybe I needed to use my creative problem-solving skills to help her with this part.

And then I had the perfect idea. "Why don't you bake her an apology?" I said. "With frosting?"

Aunt Becky froze.

Great-Uncle Timothy looked up.

I just waited. Clearly, it was a great plan. But if Aunt Becky didn't like it and wanted to try something else instead, fine. I'd still cheer her on, like I was supposed to.

She didn't smile, but she didn't say no, either. Instead, she stared out through the front window again, like she could see something that wasn't the cars driving by or the dry cleaner's across the street.

I didn't rush her. No one likes to be rushed when they're thinking about important things. So I just thought my own thoughts, about what an apology would taste like. Even Ms. Davis and I had never thought about that before.

Suddenly, Aunt Becky looked at me and smiled. "Coconut cupcakes with lime curd." She folded her arms, like it was obvious.

It wasn't obvious to me. But honestly, I didn't really care

what kind of apology she baked, so long as she got going on it. "Okay," I said. "Do you need to do research or go to the store?"

But she already had her secret recipe box open. She pulled out a card and put it on the counter. Then another. And another. And another. "If I turn this one into cupcakes and substitute limes for lemons and add a hint of coconut to this frosting—with toasted coconut on top? Or is that too much? And fill them like this . . ."

I went over so I could see. She had recipes for coconut cake and lemon curd and cream-cheese frosting, and instructions for how to fill cupcakes. Cards were spread out all over the counter.

Aunt Becky didn't remind me of a trapped princess now. She was muttering and cackling like a sorceress making up a new spell.

I glanced over at Great-Uncle Timothy to see if this seemed normal to him or if we should do something. But he was busy drawing on one of the bakery bags.

Well, if he wasn't going to be nervous about Aunt Becky forgetting about the mixer and the oven while she turned cupcakes into frogs or whatever, neither was I. "Let me know if you need any help," I told her.

A couple of people peered through the front window, probably to see if Great-Aunt Alta had left yet, and then came in.

"Welcome to our bakery!" I told them. "Today's specials

are blueberry bran muffins with ginger, and banana bread with chocolate chips."

One of the ladies sagged, all disappointed. "No jam bars?"

"Yeah, we have those, too," I told her. We really had to find a way to tell people what was happening. "How many do you want?"

She beamed at me. "Four!"

Great-Uncle Timothy rang her up while I helped the next lady, who wanted four, too.

My stomach rumbled. We still had bread and peanut butter, so I could make us some sandwiches again. We needed a better plan for tomorrow, though.

TIME GOES FAST WHEN YOU'RE HELPING PEOPLE. ABOUT TWENTY CUStomers later, I heard the Enormous Mixer of Danger start up.

Maybe ten customers after that, this amazing smell of warm coconut and fresh lime snuck out of the oven and hovered around. The customers started asking what that was, and if they could have some of it.

I shook my head. "That's Aunt Becky's special research project. Maybe if you're lucky, she'll consider selling some tomorrow."

Aunt Becky didn't say anything all afternoon. It was a little weird. Then again, so was everything else about my relatives. When we ran out of the new muffins and cookies and banana bread and it was time to close, she was still working.

So Great-Uncle Timothy wrote out a grocery list while I watched Aunt Becky squeeze wobbly white swirls of frosting out of a bag and onto her new cupcakes.

Finally, she set the bag down. She passed me an extra-wobbly cupcake. "Try this, and tell me what you think."

I peeled off the paper and took a huge bite. The bright lime of the filling that was hidden inside the coconut cake kind of exploded in my mouth. The smooth cream-cheese icing brought it all together and made it taste like happiness. "It's perfect," I told Aunt Becky.

I got a bakery box ready. But when I set it on the counter for her, she didn't move. She just stood there, staring at her cupcakes.

"Are you okay?" I asked.

When she looked up, her eyes were wide. "I can't— What if—" Her words stopped, as if she couldn't make her voice go anymore.

I knew that feeling. "Does it feel like your blood turned into lava?"

She nodded.

"Here's the thing," I explained. "Lava is more than a thousand degrees. That's way hotter than your veins can handle. So, if your blood was actually lava, it would burn right through you, and through the floor, and through the earth's surface. And we wouldn't be having this conversation."

Aunt Becky just kept staring at me. But I know that sometimes it's hard to talk when your blood feels that way.

So I went on, helping her the way Ms. Davis helps me. "Whatever it is, we can make a plan together. Only, I need to know what's up. What can't you do?"

Aunt Becky stared at the cupcakes again.

"You made the cupcakes and frosted them and everything, so it isn't that," I said. "Do you want me to put them in the box for you? Or would you rather do that yourself?" I know that you can't just go around doing things for people when they're dealing with their lava-blood and they're in no condition to stop you if they don't want you doing that. You have to ask. And you have to be patient and wait while they get themselves together enough to tell you. But breaking things down into smaller questions can help.

Aunt Becky took a deep, shuddery breath. "I can put them in the box."

I waited quietly while she did it. "Nice work," I said as she closed the lid. "Now take a deep breath in—hold it—and out." Everyone knows air cools lava off.

I tried to think what the next small step was. "Do you know where your friend lives?" I asked. "Or do we need to find that out first?"

Aunt Becky looked up at me. Her eyes were big and wild again. "I can't see her. What if—" She stopped.

I frowned. "Like, because you don't know where she lives? Or because you're too nervous? Or because she's dangerous or not healthy for you to be around? Is she the kind of friend who's mean to you or something?"

Aunt Becky just stared at me, and I sighed. Fairy-godperson stuff was harder than it looked.

Then Great-Uncle Timothy came over. He handed a long strip of paper to Aunt Becky.

He'd drawn a cartoon. There was a big question mark at the beginning. Then there was a picture of him and me driving to somebody's house. Some lady was waiting inside, looking sad. I got out of the car and took the box up to the lady. I had one of those big bubbles coming out of my mouth that said, "From Becky!" The lady took the box and smiled. Then Great-Uncle Timothy and I drove back to our bakery, and Aunt Becky smiled, too. He'd drawn the bakery cases full of cupcakes, or maybe muffins, and the oven had a big exclamation point above it, like she'd been baking something new and exciting while we were gone.

"Works for me," I said. My

blood didn't turn into lava when I thought about giving the box to Aunt Becky's sad friend, and she didn't look dangerous in the picture. Besides, Great-Uncle Timothy would be right there if anything went wrong. He seemed pretty reliable, as long as it didn't involve talking. "Is this plan okay with you, Aunt Becky?"

She stared at the paper a moment longer. Then she looked up and nodded.

"Do you want to make an 'I'm sorry' card to go with them? Or should I explain they're an apology or something?" I asked.

She shook her head, looking tired. "She'll know exactly what they mean."

"Are you positive?" I asked.

She nodded.

Well, I wasn't so sure about that. But I was supposed to be helping her help herself, not telling her how to do it. "Do you want to test another new recipe while we're gone?" I asked. Because sometimes even when all you can think about is the lava in your blood, your very favorite things can distract you a little.

She reached for her secret recipe box automatically. Great-Uncle Timothy and I waited patiently while she looked through it. I could see her shoulders calming down a little, and I knew her blood was cooling back down, too.

She pulled out a card and handed it to me. "Magic Cookie Bars," it said.

I smiled. "My friend Julia will love these. Are you going to be okay here by yourself? Do you have everything you need?"

She nodded. So I picked up the box of cupcakes and followed Great-Uncle Timothy out of the bakery.

GREAT-UNCLE TIMOTHY DROVE SLOWLY, CAREFULLY, AND IN TOTAL silence. Kind of like he does everything. Maybe he was more of a faithful horse than an old king?

I wasn't in the mood to sit there quietly with my thoughts, though. So I told him about how we needed to figure out a way for people to know what they could buy at the bakery.

"I guess we can fix the sign over the counter eventually, but I don't know how," I said. Maybe we could peel the rest of the old letters off, and get more so we could spell out something new? Or turn the board around and use the back, if we could get it down from the ceiling? It seemed like kind of a big project. "I don't think Aunt Becky's done trying new things yet, so maybe we should wait. At least, I hope she isn't."

Great-Uncle Timothy didn't say anything, but I could tell he was listening.

"If we got some big pieces of paper, we could make a new poster every day and put it in the window," I went on. "But that would be sort of wasteful."

Great-Uncle Timothy nodded. I guess he didn't have anything to add to that.

"We need something like my teacher's whiteboard or—" I stopped. It was perfect. I turned to Great-Uncle Timothy and grinned.

He didn't tell me to go on. But he raised one bushy white eyebrow. I was starting to understand that that was his way of asking.

"We could make a chalk sign for the sidewalk, like the barbershop has!" I said. "Then you could write out the bakery specials for the day, and maybe draw some pictures. What do you think?"

He stared at the road with a funny look on his face.

"I could write on it, if you don't want to," I said. "But I'm pretty busy with other stuff right now. And since you like making art, maybe you want to take this on?"

He glanced at me and gave me one of his sudden, real smiles—the kind that happens so fast I feel like I could have imagined it. Only, why would I be smiling back?

Then he pulled over and parked in front of a little white house with a purple door and a beautiful garden, all full of flowers. He pointed to the box in my lap and then to the door.

"Got it," I said.

I knew my line from the cartoon. So I got out of the car, walked up the pretty path, and rang the doorbell.

A lady about Aunt Becky's age answered. She wasn't all faded and tired, like Aunt Becky—she had makeup on and was wearing a dress with flowers. Something about her didn't look that happy, though.

"Are you selling something?" she asked.

I shook my head. "These are from Becky," I told her, and handed her the box. "She said you'd understand." It felt like I should say something more. But that wasn't the plan. "Bye."

When I got back in the car, I saw she was still standing there, staring at me, holding the box.

That was okay. People need some time to think when someone apologizes, especially if they weren't expecting it. And she hadn't even tasted one of the apology cupcakes yet, so she probably didn't have a clue. But she would.

8

THAT NIGHT, EVERYONE was pretty quiet. Well, except for Great-Aunt Alta. She wasn't yelling, though—just tapping her fingers on the table and sulking. *Tap . . . tap . . . tap . . . tap-tap. Tap-tap-tap-tap-tap-tap. . . . Tap . . . tap . . . tap . . . tap-tap . . .*

I pretended not to notice. I knew Ms. Davis would tell her she was way too old to behave like that, and to sort her stuff out instead of holding it in, because it wouldn't be pretty when she finally exploded. But I'd had a long day already. I'd met my new fairy godperson and maybe a new friend, helped Aunt Becky with her ridiculous fight and her lava-blood, and even thought up something for Great-Uncle Timothy. That was plenty. Great-Aunt Alta could wait, as long as she wasn't causing problems for anyone else. Besides, I had a whole stack of new library books to read.

After dinner, I helped Great-Uncle Timothy clear the plates from the table, scrape them off, and load the dishwasher. When we were finished, he smiled at me. Then he unlocked and opened the back door that led out to the garden.

"Where are you going?" I asked. "Can I come, too?"

He smiled again and nodded, so I followed him out.

We walked down a short, straight path between some vegetable beds, through the soft light of evening. It looked kind of like the garden at my school, except the lettuce and tomatoes and beans were in perfectly straight rows, and there wasn't any art or flowers. Nothing except a bunch of wind chimes—not just one set but eight or nine, all swinging from a tree, playing sad songs to themselves.

"Why do you have so many wind chimes?" I asked.

But he just sighed and glanced back at the house.

At the end of the path was a small shed, with a padlock on the door. Great-Uncle Timothy pulled his keys out of his pocket and unlocked it. He opened the door and stepped through, turning on a light.

I followed him inside.

A battery-powered lantern sat on a workbench, glowing yellow, just bright enough to see by. I stared all around me, as quiet as Great-Uncle Timothy, for once. It was like stepping into a magic land. Mysterious bits of wood and wire covered the workbench, along with jars stuffed with paintbrushes and paper towels streaked with paint. A row of tools hung above it, outlined on the pegboard behind them. Above that, the wall was covered in tiny paintings—people, animals, trees, houses—all mixed together like a comic book had broken through the page and spilled out into this strange world.

I couldn't tell if the other walls had pictures on them, too. Pieces of plywood, lumber, and chicken wire were leaning up against them, all shapes and sizes.

"Wow," I whispered. It felt like if anyone caught me inside there, I'd be sent back to the real world, where I belonged. And I didn't want that—not yet. "This is amazing."

Great-Uncle Timothy grinned at me. He dragged a couple of sawhorses out into the small room. He rubbed his chin, then flipped through a stack of plywood, stopping to pull out a piece. He set it on the sawhorses and waved me back toward the doorway.

I watched from there as he measured and marked the wood. "Wait! Are you building a sign—like the one I told you about?"

He grinned at me again, kind of shyly. Something in my heart sprouted and grew, making me feel as warm as Aunt Becky's new muffins. Slowly, he sawed through the wood with an old handsaw that could have come straight out of fairy-tale times. From a woodcutter, perhaps, living by himself in a tiny cabin deep in the dark woods?

"Does this mean yes, you want to do it?" I asked him. "You don't have to, if you don't want to. I won't be mad."

"Yes," Great-Uncle Timothy whispered, and smiled.

It was clear he'd done stuff like this before. He didn't have to stop and look anything up when he got out the sandpaper or added the hinges.

"Should we paint it, do you think?" I asked, inspecting the cans of spray paint overflowing a crate under the workbench.

He shrugged, doubt coming back into his face.

"I'll research it at the library tomorrow," I told him.

He nodded, smiling again. I'd never seen him smile this much.

"Thanks for showing me your secret hideout," I said, smiling back. "I'm glad you have somewhere to do your art."

When he was finished, we carried the sign around the house and loaded it into the trunk of the car. As I followed him through the dark garden and back inside the gloomy old house, the glowing yellow shed felt farther and farther away. It was good, but it wasn't enough, I decided. Great-Uncle Timothy needed to be able to do his art where everyone could see it, not just in secret.

Aunt Becky and Great-Aunt Alta were sitting in the living room in silence. Aunt Becky was writing something in a notebook—probably recipe ideas, I thought. Great-Aunt Alta was staring at the curtains over the window like she had X-ray vision, her fingers still tapping away on the arm of her chair.

Well, if they wanted to be quiet, that was fine with me; I had plenty of books to read. Before I opened my book, though, I slipped Aunt Becky a note. It said: "Can we make

pizza tomorrow? I think we should have some real food for lunch."

AUNT BECKY SEEMED ALMOST HAPPY WHEN WE GOT TO THE BAKERY the next morning. She mixed some pizza dough even before she mixed the blueberry-bran-muffin batter, because she said the pizza dough had to sit for a while to let the yeast do its thing before we could do anything with it. And I guess she forgot all about her usual blueberry muffins, because she moved right on to her favorite cookies. I didn't see any reason to remind her, since no one wanted to buy the old boring stuff anyway. Pretty soon she had all four ovens going, and a mixer full of coconut-cupcake batter. I watched while she cut up the magic cookie bars she'd made yesterday. They had chocolate chips and coconut and who knows what else, and they looked delicious.

She seemed fine for now. So I moved on to observing Great-Uncle Timothy.

He was filling one of the white cloth funnel bags with chocolate frosting from a big bowl. It had a metal tip with a design cut out. When he'd gotten all the frosting inside, he twisted the top shut, then held it over the first chocolate cupcake.

He squeezed the bag. Frosting started oozing out. Then he swirled the frosting around the top of the cupcake, just like the ones at the grocery store.

"That's so cool!" I said. "Can I try?"

He nodded and handed me the bag. It was heavier than it looked, and hard to control with my enormous gloves on. I tried to swirl it just like he did, but it looked more like a wobbly mess. I could feel my face burn. "I'm sorry," I said. "I thought I could do it. I didn't mean to mess it up."

But he just ran a butter knife over the top of the cupcake, sweeping it clean again. Then he put the cupcake back down in front of me.

"I didn't know you could erase cupcakes like that!" I said, starting to slowly squeeze the frosting out again. This time, I thought I was getting the hang of it.

Great-Uncle Timothy grinned at me.

"Do you like decorating cupcakes?" I asked him.

His smile faded. He shrugged and took the top off a container of yellow sprinkles. Carefully, he picked up a pinch between his gloved fingers and let it rain down over the chocolate frosting.

I watched him work, thinking about his secret world in the shed. "Do you like doing all kinds of art?" I asked him. "Or do you like drawing best?"

He smiled. He smoothed out the leftover frosting in the bowl and scratched "ALL" into it with the tip of the knife.

Then he wiped the letters away, like he couldn't bear to look at them.

I thought of him being stuck in the bakery for hours

every day. What had he been dreaming of while Aunt Becky thought about blueberry bran muffins with ginger?

BY THE TIME WE UNLOCKED THE DOOR, THE WHOLE BAKERY SMELLED like coconut and lime. It made me happy . . . right up until the moment that Kevin from the library walked in. He was holding a pink box, and he didn't look happy at all.

"Hi, Kevin," I said loudly.

Aunt Becky looked up from the mixer. She froze.

"Hey, Fiona. Hey, Tim," Kevin said. He tried to smile. "These are for you, Becky. From Annie." He set the box on the counter and backed away, like it might explode.

"Do you want a muffin?" I asked. I wasn't sure what was going on.

For a minute, he reminded me of a kid stuck at the top of the high diving board, peering down at the pool below, with a whole line of people on the ladder behind him. And then he nodded. "Yes," he said very firmly. "I would like a muffin. One of the good ones, please." He looked at me like he was trying to send me a message with his mind. "I got some new books in yesterday—you should come by later, if you can." Then he paid for his muffin and left, fast.

We all stared at the pink box for a while. "I think you should open it," I said. It's better to know what's going on, even when it makes you nervous.

Aunt Becky crept up on the box like something might jump out and bite her. She opened the lid. Then she reached inside and pulled out a perfect little pie, only about as big as her hand. She held it up so we could see.

The smell wafting toward me was familiar, almost. Warm, sweet, nutty, a little tart . . . I realized what it was. "Your friend made your favorite cookies?" I asked. "Only, as cute little pies? Is that her apology? That's good, right?"

But Aunt Becky's face was thunderous. She turned the pie so I could see the top. Floating amid the raspberry jam was a piece of dough, cut in the shape of a sword. It was super detailed, with a groove running down the blade and a design scratched into the hilt, like twisted metal. It even had a fancy little frosting sparkle on the tip.

"No," she said. "It's a declaration of war." She set the pie down and rushed to her secret recipe box.

"Whoa, whoa, whoa!" I said, following her. "You're apologizing, remember? How is a pastry war going to help you be friends again?" I folded my arms and gave her the look

Ms. Davis gives me when I'm not being entirely truthful with myself. (I know I got it right, too. I have practiced that look a *lot* in the mirror.)

But Aunt Becky didn't even glance up.

I DECIDED I'D BETTER GET SOME MORE INFORMATION BEFORE THINGS got out of hand. So I went to the library.

"What's going on?" I asked Kevin as soon as I walked in. "Why is your sister sending Aunt Becky pies with swords? Is she still mad? Can't you tell her to get over it?" I really did not have time to be some other lady's fairy godperson, too. Somebody else needed to step up here.

Kevin sighed. "I think she'd gotten over it and was just staying away out of habit. But then she decided that your aunt was trying to outdo her cupcakes."

I blinked. "*What?* Those were supposed to be Aunt Becky's apology!"

"Well, coconut is Annie's favorite," Kevin said thoughtfully. "She's been making and selling coconut cupcakes in her bakery for years. They're beautiful—they're covered in flowers and sparkly sugar. The problem is . . ." He looked around the library. No one else was there. Then he whispered, "Becky's taste better."

I was still processing all this. "Your sister has a bakery, too?"

He nodded.

"And you're sure Aunt Becky knows about her bakery, and that she makes coconut cupcakes, and all that?"

He nodded again.

"I need to send an email," I told him.

Dear Fiona,

I'm committed to sending your lessons for the whole summer, wherever you are. But I don't think you should plan on coming home right away. I feel like your mom might be a little too optimistic about how quickly she'll be done. The people running her program have a lot of practice helping people with their addictions. They've said to plan for her to spend the summer there, so that's what I'm planning.

I'm glad to hear you're settling in. Now, tell me more about this girl Julia. Is she a reader, too?

Sincerely,
Nia Davis

P.S. I know it can be hard to talk about mixed-up feelings. But it's fine to tell your mom all of what you're feeling, not just some of it. Her feelings and her worries are not more important than yours. Sure, she might not like hearing some of it. But she's got people helping her with her own mixed-up feelings, and she's stronger than you think. She can take it.

Dear Ms. Davis,

That's good to know, I guess. I am still fine. But things are a little messed up here.

Aunt Becky was making some amazing new recipes, even though her mom yelled at her about it. (Don't worry, I told Great-Aunt Alta that I don't like yelling and that she should find a better way. Mr. Rivera said I did a great job. He was there, so he should know.)

Anyway, Aunt Becky finally told me what's really wrong. You're not going to believe this, but she had an argument with her friend way back before I was born. About frosting! Apparently it was important to her. She didn't know how to apologize, maybe because it was so long ago. I could see that words weren't playing to her strengths, so I said maybe she should bake an apology. So she made these delicious coconut-lime cupcakes! Great-Uncle Timothy and I delivered them for her. That part all went fine.

But instead of calling her up and talking it out or baking her own apology or whatever, that lady sent back pies with swords. (Just between you and me, they're pretty cool swords.) Now they're at war, I guess. It's just like you always say: people don't really think things through when they're mad.

If you have any advice, I'd like to hear it.

Your apprentice-fairy-godperson-in-training,
Fiona

P.S. Do you ever get annoyed with the people you help? Like: Come on, people, I just helped you! How come you have to mess everything up again?

P.P.S. Since you might need some time to reply, I'm going to call my new friend, Julia, and see what she thinks. Yeah, she's a reader, too. She's going to be a witch. Or maybe she already is one. So she should have some ideas.

P.P.P.S. I guess Mom didn't have time to email me today. Probably she's really busy with all the stuff she has to learn. Or maybe she forgot.

Dear Mom,

How are you? I hope you are learning a lot. I guess you must be pretty busy there.

I'm learning a lot, too. Aunt Becky taught me how to make a new kind of cookie that you cut up into bars. You'd like them.

I am fine. I miss you.

Love,
Fiona

9

KEVIN WAS STILL looking unhappy when I finished my email.

"Do you think your sister poisoned those pies?" I asked him. "Do I need to throw them out, just in case?" Maybe his sister wanted to be a witch, too—the "Snow White" kind.

He looked a little startled, but he shook his head right away. "No! She might be mad at Becky, but she wouldn't hurt anyone."

I thought about it. Aunt Becky wouldn't poison anyone, either. At least, not with something she baked. It would probably be bad for her bakery. "I'm sorry things got messed up," I told Kevin.

"I'm sorry, too," he said. "Sometimes people just have to sort things out their own way, I guess."

I was pretty sure that if I hadn't come here, Aunt Becky would never, ever have done anything but bake boring cookies for the rest of her life. So I didn't see how she was going to fix this without me. It was just that I didn't really have a plan yet for how to help.

I got Julia's phone number out of my backpack. "Can I use the phone?"

Kevin pushed some buttons until he got a dial tone. He slid the phone over to me.

I dialed the number.

"Hello, this is Ernesto Rivera speaking."

"This is Fiona," I said. "Don't call 911. This isn't an emergency. I'm fine."

"Nice to hear from you, Fiona. What's up?"

He didn't sound like he was in a hurry, so I explained about the sword pies. "Ms. Davis says sometimes it helps you get your thoughts in order and figure out your plan when you talk it over with someone," I told him. "So I thought maybe . . . Can Julia come down to the library? If she wants to? She doesn't have to."

"Hang on a sec and I'll ask her," he said.

I waited, and after a minute he came back on. "She says she'd love to hang out. How about in half an hour? I can drop my niece's bike off for you then, too."

"That works," I told him. "Thanks." I gave Kevin back the phone and went to check my email again.

Dear Fiona,

I was going to type that I'm sorry things aren't going as smoothly as you'd hoped. But you know what? That's not true. There's no "perfect" in this world, and things rarely go smoothly. I'd rather help you learn to cope with that now, while you're learning about helping people, than leave you to figure it out on your own later on.

People get stuck in their ways, even ways that aren't working for them. When they first get unstuck, life might feel easier, or they might pretend it does. But sometimes it's not that simple. Sometimes they feel like everything's falling apart for a while. When that happens, people might grab hold of anything that feels familiar, even if they know it's not a good idea. Things might get worse before they get better, until they truly believe it's time for a change. Sometimes that's the only way they can pick up the pieces and try something new. Something that might work better.

See, this work that we're doing—helping people—it's not easy. Not even when you've had a lot of training and practice. Sure, you can tell people what to do, like a king in one of those stories of yours. Doesn't mean they have to listen. Trying to figure out how to help people help themselves is another thing altogether.

Remember, just because this took an unexpected turn

doesn't mean you didn't learn anything from it. So you know what? I think you're ready for your next lesson.

FAIRY-GODPERSON TRAINING: LESSON 2

1. *Find a situation you don't feel good about.*
2. *Discover your truth—what you really think, not what someone else thinks you should think.*
3. *Speak your truth. You might tell it to the person in the situation. Or you might find someone else to tell—someone you trust who might be able to help. Or someone you could ask for advice.*
4. *Observe what happens when you wield the power of your truth. It might not be what you think will happen. But you can still learn something from it.*

There's no rush on this lesson. But you can't learn to do what you need to do until you learn to say what you need to say.

Sincerely,
Nia Davis

P.S. Yeah, I know, you've done this before. But practice helps.

P.P.S. I'm sorry your mom hasn't emailed you yet today. But the work she's doing really does take time and effort.

My advice is to keep saying what you need to tell her, just like we've practiced—including that you love her.

P.P.P.S. Here's my truth: next time you email me, I'd like to hear more about how you're doing. Something more than "I am still fine," please.

10

AFTER THAT, KEVIN helped me find some books about how to do fancy writing for Great-Uncle Timothy. I knew he could do the art, but we were going to need some words, too. So we found a book on calligraphy, which turns out to be really swirly writing; one on graffiti art, with cool blocky lettering; and one on chalkboard art for parties. I wasn't sure if any of them were really Great-Uncle Timothy's style, but at least he'd know that I wanted to support his art.

We were just finishing our research on how to make a chalkboard sign when Julia and her dad arrived, right when they said they would. Julia's bike helmet had a little black witch's hat stuck to it. I was pretty impressed.

"Hey, Fiona," Mr. Rivera said. "How are things in sword-pie land?"

I shrugged. "Fine, I guess. Kevin says they're not poisoned."

"Glad to hear it," Mr. Rivera said. He grinned at Kevin and clapped him on the shoulder. "Hang in there, man."

Kevin shook his head, but at least he smiled back.

"Are you ready to check out your new wheels?" Mr. Rivera asked me.

"Yeah, let's go somewhere!" Julia said. "Marisol says you can't put anything disgusting in her bike basket and you have to promise to always lock it up through the frame and the wheels. We've got her lock and her helmet."

I told Kevin thanks for the help and followed them out to Mr. Rivera's car. Julia went around the back to get the bikes out. "The yellow one is Marisol's—that's the one you're borrowing," she said.

Mr. Rivera helped me get the seat to the right height and tighten the straps on the helmet. He checked to make sure the helmet didn't wiggle, then gave me a thumbs-up. "Looks like you're all set," he said. "Do you have everything you need?"

I nodded. "Tell your niece thanks for letting me borrow her bike."

"I will," he said. "You two have fun. Call me if you need anything."

"Bye, Dad!" Julia said. She turned to me. "Dad said you had something you wanted to talk through. Want to go to the park? It's only a little ways away."

So we rode over, parked our bikes on the grass in the sunshine, and plopped down beside them. There were a bunch of kids playing soccer nearby and little kids screaming on the playground, but we had this part to ourselves.

Julia picked some dandelion flowers. "So, what's up?"

I watched as she pinched a stem between her fingernails to make a slit near the end. She poked the stem of another one through it and did the same thing to its stem. "I've been helping Aunt Becky with a problem she has." I explained about the really old fight, and my idea, and Aunt Becky's deep dive into coconut-lime cupcakes.

"The bakery near my house makes coconut cupcakes," Julia said. "They have white cake and sparkly pink frosting and coconut all around the edge, kind of like a border, I guess, and then frosting flowers in different colors in the middle."

"Wow, fancy," I said. I didn't think Aunt Becky could do anything like that. "I guess that's her friend—enemy—her frenemy's bakery?" I told her about the sword pies and what Kevin had said about his sister being mad.

"Weird." Julia tied the end of the last dandelion stem around the first one, and dropped it over her head like a necklace. "If you had been mad at someone for that long, what kind of bakery apology would you want?"

"Maybe oatmeal cookies with chocolate chips? They're my favorite. But I wouldn't stay mad at someone for that long. That's just silly." I tried to think about how that could even happen.

In the back of my mind, I remembered my mom pulling a pan of my favorite cookies out of the oven. She was smiling at me kind of anxiously, the way she did when things got better for a while. I shook my head to make the picture go away. That wasn't the same sort of situation at all. "What about you?"

"Well, witches can definitely stay mad at someone for a long time," she said. "Of course, some fights are partly their fault. Witches aren't perfect, especially not bad witches. And if it was partly my fault, I wouldn't want the apology to be too big and too perfect—you know?"

I nodded. It was a good point. "I'm not a witch, though," I told her. "I'm training to be a fairy godperson so I can help people."

"Who's teaching you?" she asked. "Are you learning from a book or something?"

I explained about Ms. Davis, and how she'd finally agreed to send me some lessons. "Your dad's probably pretty good at this stuff, too," I told her. "But Ms. Davis and I have been talking about it for years." That reminded me of a question I'd been meaning to ask her. "What's *your* favorite kind of cookie?"

"Chocolate-dipped coconut macaroons," she said immediately. "That bakery I told you about—I mean, don't get me wrong, your aunt's new cookies are amazing—but that's the one we usually go to. Last Halloween, they made these coconut macaroons that were tall and pointy, and they dipped the bottom part in chocolate and left a little puddle at the bottom, and when they dried, they were almost exactly like a witch's hat! Not a good witch's hat or a bad witch's hat— both." She grinned. "Just like me."

I grinned back. Those did sound like the perfect cookies for Julia.

"So, what will your aunt do now?" Julia asked, picking more dandelions and starting another chain.

I sighed. "Probably make everything worse," I admitted. "I guess she's really bad at apologizing."

"Is she going to call her frenemy up and yell at her or something?"

"Nah," I said. "She's going to bake something. I just don't know what."

Julia got up and dropped the second chain over my head. She held out her hands. "Well, it will probably be delicious," she said. "Let's go see!"

I let her pull me to my feet.

We stopped to check out the barbershop's sign on our way to the bakery. I told Julia how Great-Uncle Timothy had built one, and now all we needed was special chalkboard paint.

"The hardware store probably has some," Julia said. "We can ride there next, if you want." She studied the sign. "Your great-uncle could definitely draw something better than that. Unless that's supposed to be Mr. Potato Head?"

I frowned. "Maybe Great-Uncle Timothy could do their sign, too, after he's had some practice."

But Julia was already wheeling her bike down the sidewalk. "Come on!"

The bakery smelled amazing. Not sweet this time, but . . . I grinned at Julia in relief. "Aunt Becky's making pizza!" Not war. Just pizza.

"Fifteen minutes till lunch," Aunt Becky called out, glancing up from where she was putting something on little disks of dough.

Julia went back behind the counter to see what she was up to. I followed, grabbing aprons and gloves and shower caps for both of us.

"What's that supposed to be?" Julia asked.

"Flaming swords," Aunt Becky said, balancing a piece of red pepper on a slice of mushroom.

I frowned. Okay, maybe pizza *and* war.

"Are you sure?" Julia asked. "I thought swords were supposed to look a little more . . . sword-y."

I examined the mushrooms more closely. Julia was right. Maybe Aunt Becky's frenemy wouldn't even notice them. "Kevin says his sister thinks you're trying to outdo her cupcakes," I said. "She didn't realize they were an apology. So maybe you should try again—a different way this time."

Aunt Becky didn't look very surprised. I noticed she didn't say anything about how that wasn't what she'd meant to do at all, either. She just added a mushroom sword to the next mini-pizza.

I tried again. "Maybe you could send her a card or flowers or something. Or you could just call her. I mean, I know it's scary. But you want this to get fixed—right? This fight was making you sad."

No response. It was like trying to talk to someone who was reading the exciting part of a book.

I sighed and kept trying. "Are these her favorites, too?"

"No." Aunt Becky plopped a red pepper on top. It fell off its mushroom and slid down into the cheese and sauce. More cheese fell on top of it. "These are *my* favorites."

Julia looked at me. I shrugged. I couldn't exactly tell Aunt Becky not to make her own favorites.

Aunt Becky didn't notice. Well, there were plenty of other people to help while I figured out what she was up to now. And those pizzas did smell good. "Can Julia stay for lunch?"

Aunt Becky nodded, still hard at work.

"Want to help some customers until they're ready?" I asked Julia.

"Sure!" she said.

I helped her put everything on, and she tied my apron for me.

"We need a picture of our matching looks," Julia said, posing like a fashion model in her shower cap. "Will you take a picture of us?" She handed her phone to Aunt Becky.

Aunt Becky blinked, like she didn't know where we'd come from or when we got there. But she took the phone.

Julia and I put our heads together and grinned at her. Then I did a fairy-godperson pose, using a wooden spoon for my magic wand, and Julia did a witch pose, with one of my library books as a spell book.

In between customers, I told Great-Uncle Timothy about the chalkboard paint. "After lunch, Julia and I are going to go to the hardware store and see if they have some."

He pulled a beat-up wallet out of his pocket and counted out ten one-dollar bills.

"Thanks," I said, tucking them into my pocket. I still had the money Mom gave me. But I was glad he wanted to be part of helping himself.

"I got you some books from the library about how to do fancy writing," I told him, in case he wasn't sure about that part.

He glanced at me and gave me another of his sudden,

real smiles. Then he folded one of the index cards Aunt Becky uses for her recipes in half, with the boring white side out, like a sidewalk sign, and started drawing on it while the next guy figured out what he wanted.

I left him to it and showed Julia how to help people.

When the timer went off, Great-Uncle Timothy passed me his drawing. It was covered in tiny pictures of muffins and cookies and cupcakes, and fancy writing that said what they were.

"That'll be perfect," I told him, smiling.

Aunt Becky took the first batch of her flaming-sword mini-pizzas out of the oven. My stomach growled. But she wasn't focused on lunch. "Uncle Timothy, I need you and Fiona to deliver these to Annie."

I hesitated. I could tell Aunt Becky no, I wouldn't help her anymore. Not if she was going to keep fighting instead of trying to apologize for real. But then she wouldn't have anybody. How would that be better? I was supposed to practice speaking my truths, but I wasn't even sure what they were. Did I really want to tell her all that?

Not really, I decided. I went over so I could talk to Aunt Becky privately. Julia followed me. Great-Uncle Timothy raised his eyebrow at the next customer.

"If Great-Uncle Timothy and I leave, who's going to help everyone while we're gone?" I asked.

Aunt Becky looked up, puzzled. She saw the line of customers and frowned. Sometimes I think she forgets bakeries are supposed to sell stuff.

"I could go with Fiona. We could take them on our bikes," Julia offered. "I know how to get to Annie's bakery."

My stomach grumbled. "I think we should have lunch first." I still didn't want to be part of this. But I didn't have a better idea.

"Okay!" Julia said. "Let's have flaming-sword pizzas. Then we can ride to the bakery and deliver some to Annie. We could go to the hardware store after that—it's not far." She grinned.

"Fine." Aunt Becky sliced up a couple of her pizzas, put them on plates, and handed them to us, with napkins. Then she went back to the next batch of flaming swords.

The pizza was delicious. But I didn't feel good eating it. Part of it was that I was nervous about delivering flaming swords, even if they were only pizza. What if Aunt Becky's frenemy yelled at me?

Another part of it was that I still didn't know how everything had gone so wrong so fast. Or if it was all my fault. What kind of fairy godperson went around starting wars without meaning to?

But as I put the bakery box into the bike basket, Julia didn't seem nervous at all. Maybe she didn't know what she was getting into.

"Are you okay?" she asked. "You got really quiet."

I paid attention to my breathing so that maybe my blood wouldn't decide it was lava. "I don't really like it when people yell."

"Neither does my dad," she said cheerfully.

"Really?" I said. Mr. Rivera hadn't seemed like his blood ever turned into lava.

"Yeah, he just has to work through it," she said. "Is this sharing time or something? Okay. I don't really like raisins."

"Got it," I said. "I just—I don't really know how this is going to go."

Julia shrugged. "That's because you're not a princess. Princesses wait for something to happen, and princes do what they're told. But witches and fairy godpeople try something and see what happens next." She snapped her helmet on. "Ready?"

Not really. But I wasn't going to wait around like a princess while Julia helped people. I climbed on the bike. "Ready."

ANNIE'S BAKERY WAS PRETTY. I KNOW ABOUT GINGERBREAD HOUSES, though, so I didn't trust it. But maybe Aunt Becky's frenemy spent more time baking than plotting against her. (And if a not-so-bad witch who really liked gingerbread wanted to do something useful with her cooking skills and didn't want to go into construction, well . . . a bakery could be a good place to start.)

Julia stopped in front of a white-painted bike rack. She locked her bike and took off her helmet, foofing out her hair. "Come on!"

My stomach dropped a little further as we walked up to the pink door. I didn't know this lady, and I didn't want her to think I was her enemy. But I did have a new lesson to work on. I hadn't spoken my truths to Aunt Becky, but maybe I didn't have to. Maybe I could tell the other person in this situation instead. There was at least one thing I thought this lady should know.

So I followed Julia in, carrying Aunt Becky's bakery box.

11

JULIA WALKED RIGHT up to the glass bakery case. "I'm going to have a macaroon," she said. "Want one? My treat."

I hesitated, and she turned to look at me. "Wait—do you hate coconut?"

I could see Aunt Becky's frenemy behind the counter, but she was busy talking to a customer. "I'm not sure I should."

"It's just a cookie," Julia said. "I'm getting two. If you don't want yours, I'll save it for later."

"Okay," I said quietly. "Thanks."

The lady in front of us took her box and left. I followed Julia up to the register, trying to breathe in, and out.

"Hey, Annie," Julia said, like it was any other day. "This is my new friend, Fiona."

Annie nodded at Julia and gave me a look. "You're staying with the Starkes. Kevin told me about you. He says you're a reader."

I nodded. Time to speak my truth. "The apology cupcakes I delivered were my idea," I said. "I didn't mean to make you mad."

Annie raised an eyebrow. " 'Apology cupcakes,' huh? Tell me: Why did she pick my favorite kind? Why outdo me in front of the whole town?" She folded her arms. "An apology is when you say you're wrong, you learned something, and you'll try to do better next time. Those weren't an apology. They were an 'I told you so.' "

She had a point. "I'm sorry you aren't friends," I said. "It seems like you have some stuff in common. And . . ." I hesitated. "I think Aunt Becky could use a friend."

"When Becky Starke is ready to apologize, I'll listen," she said.

"Why don't you just apologize to her instead?" Julia said. "It sounds like you're better at it."

"Because I'm not the one who was wrong!" Annie replied. She sounded like she believed it, too.

Yeah, they had a *lot* in common. I sighed. "Then these are from Aunt Becky," I told her, and slid the bakery box across the counter.

She opened the box. "What are these supposed to be?"

"Pizzas," I said, just as Julia said, "Flaming swords."

"Flaming swords?" An evil-witch look came over Annie's face. She even cackled.

Julia and I exchanged glances. Julia seemed pretty excited, to be honest.

"Flaming swords . . . ," Annie muttered, turning away. "Portia, take over, please! And pack up some of my treats for these girls, on the house. Make sure they take some of *my* pizzas—ah, Becky didn't tell you who taught her to make them, did she? And some of *my* coconut cupcakes." She gave us another sort-of-evil smile.

Julia grinned. "Awesome! Thanks, Annie!"

I didn't think it was that awesome. But Annie was already hurrying into the back of the bakery. I didn't say anything.

A tall Black teenager came up to the counter. Her hair was a cool mix of blue, green, and purple, and she was wearing a white apron that was covered in pastel splotches. Icing, maybe? She nodded to Julia.

"This is my friend Fiona," Julia told her. "We're delivering these flaming-sword pizzas that her aunt made, over at the other bakery. You should try one—they're really good."

Portia examined the box that Annie had left behind. She took out one of the pizzas and turned it all around, inspecting it carefully. I wondered who she'd be in a fairy tale.

Portia put the little pizza on a plate and cut it into tiny slices, the way Aunt Becky had. She took a bite, closed her eyes, and chewed thoughtfully. Then she swallowed and opened her eyes. "Nice," she said. "The basil and oregano are on point. And that hint of cayenne at the finish really elevates the whole thing." She inspected her slice again. "A mix of red and yellow peppers would represent the flames better, though. Maybe black olives for the hilt? And she's got to cut the mushrooms into a straight line, or the effect doesn't work. You tell her I said so."

"But . . ." I hesitated. "Shouldn't you—I mean—won't you get in trouble?"

Portia laughed. "Look, I like Annie. But that doesn't mean I'm taking her side in this—whatever *this* is. I'm my own person, with my own thoughts. And I can help anybody I want to with their art."

I looked at Aunt Becky's pizza again. It wasn't what I'd call art.

But Portia wasn't done. "Those two don't just bake—they create. At least, Annie does, and I guess your aunt does, too, in her own way. That makes it not just food but art. And you can't become the kind of person who holds art back. Art is for everyone."

Julia was nodding, but I wasn't so sure. I was still recovering from getting that last truth out. And it hadn't even helped.

So instead, I changed the subject. "If you were in a fairy tale, who would you be?"

Portia took her time thinking about it. She didn't ask why I wanted to know. I could see she understood it was an important question. Finally, she smiled. "The blacksmith."

I nodded, impressed. Sometimes the blacksmith is the hero, sometimes not. They're not really on anyone's side. But they always get stuff done. "Nice to meet you," I said, and smiled back.

"What if you were a cookie?" Julia asked.

"I'm going to have to think about that one," Portia told her, grinning. "If I could fit all of me into one cookie . . . Well, it would be a masterpiece, for sure."

Julia nodded, laughing. I could see they were friends, even though they weren't the same age.

Portia put two mini-pizzas into a bakery bag and two coconut cupcakes into a box. (They did look really cool, just like Julia had described.) "No charge—boss's orders," she said, setting them down. "What else would you like?"

"Two coconut macaroons, please," Julia said immediately. "Are you going to do the witch's hat ones this fall?"

Portia laughed. "Could be," she said. "Unless we think of something even better, of course."

Julia looked skeptical, but she nodded. "What's your pick?" she asked me.

I hesitated, staring into the case. It was one thing to

accept what Annie said we had to take or what Julia chose. It was another to pick something myself.

Portia saw me thinking. "I already know Julia's a witch. So who would you be in a fairy tale?"

"The fairy godperson," I told her. It seemed like she'd understand.

She nodded slowly. "A fairy godperson who just does whatever the princess wants her to—is that it?"

I could see where she was going with this. She knew as well as I did that sometimes the fairy godperson's job is to do what's needed, even if it's not what the princess wants at all.

I stared into the case again. "Two of your chocolate chip cookies, please."

She nodded and put them into the box. Then she closed it. "Compliments of Picture Perfect Bakery," she said. "Nice to meet you, Fiona."

"Thanks, Portia!" Julia said, grabbing the box.

THERE WAS A BENCH BY THE PATH. WE SAT DOWN SO WE COULD EAT. All that biking had made some room in my stomach. Being done with the delivery without anybody yelling didn't hurt, either.

I tried one of Annie's coconut cupcakes. It was really cute . . . but without the tart lime filling, the cake part was squishy and sweet, but not that interesting. And the icing just tasted like sugar, with a little coconut on top.

"I guess that's why Annie's mad," Julia said. She stuffed the rest of her cupcake in her mouth anyway.

I nodded. Understanding it didn't help me see a way to fix it, though.

Julia swallowed. "What's wrong?"

Lots of things, I thought. I stared down the path, back where we'd come from. "I'm supposed to be learning to help people," I told her. "If Aunt Becky actually wanted to apologize, I'd help her, no problem. But maybe she doesn't. Not really."

"So don't help her." Julia smiled at me like everything was decided. "What do you want to do instead?"

"It's not about what *I* want to do," I said.

"Why not?" she asked. "What is it about?"

I shrugged. "If people don't get help, they just . . . Things get out of control."

"And the next thing you know, they're baking flaming-sword pizzas." Julia nodded. "But come on—how were you going to stop her from doing what she wanted to do? Why is that *your* job?"

"Because I'm a fairy godperson!" The words poured out of me. "I'm supposed to make things better—that's my job! But what if I can't? What if I just keep making things worse?"

"It's not like the ones in fairy tales always make things better," Julia pointed out. "I mean, I guess it depends which version you read. But I don't think walls of thorns and sleeping for a hundred years are very good solutions. And that was when some of them teamed up and made an effort to fix something." She shrugged. Then she looked at me hard, like she really had magic—witch magic or maybe friend magic. "Are you okay?"

I felt all the swirling, mixed-up feelings inside me. How could I even start trying to explain all that? And what would Julia think? I stuffed the last of the cupcake in my mouth instead of answering.

But she didn't look away. "You don't have to talk about it, if you don't want to," she said. "Just don't forget I'm your friend." She got up and stretched. "Let's go to the hardware store. You still want to get your chalkboard paint, right?"

"Right," I said, wiping all the sticky-sweet off my hands. At least Great-Uncle Timothy didn't seem to be itching for a battle.

I STAYED QUIET AS WE RODE DOWN THE BIKE PATH TO THE HARDWARE store. Julia didn't, though. She told me all about everything we passed—her favorite burger at the diner, her favorite swing on the playground, the time she accidentally locked her dad out of his car in that parking lot. It kind of calmed me down, but it also kind of made me remember I didn't really belong here.

"What do you need again?" Julia asked as we locked up the bikes.

I got the instructions Kevin had printed for me out of my backpack and checked them. "Just a can of chalkboard paint, a paint roller, and some chalk. I think the rest of this stuff is for building the sign, and that's already done."

"Got it," Julia said, and marched inside.

The hardware store was crowded with tools, like a bigger version of Great-Uncle Timothy's shed. Julia found the paint section. Then we had to read all the cans, checking for chalkboard paint. There were a *lot* of kinds of paint. But we found it in the end, tucked away on the bottom shelf, near the rollers.

When we went up front to pay, of course there was a whole chalkboard paint display near the registers, along with a sample chalkboard. It had cool swirly writing on it in three different colors of chalk. But it said "Happy Valentine's Day." Which was kind of strange for June.

Julia held up a pink marker. "Did you know they make pens that write chalk?"

An older lady with white hair, pale skin, and brown eyes came over to us. She was wearing a construction apron, and she smiled when she saw Julia. "Nice to see you. Can I help you girls with something?"

"This is my friend Fiona. She's working on a project with her great-uncle," Julia told her. "Fiona, this is Elfine."

I blurted out, "Why Valentine's Day?"

Elfine looked at the chalkboard and laughed. "Because the lady who demonstrated the chalk markers retired back in February, and none of us have attempted to redo the sign. I suppose we'll have to get someone in eventually." She turned back to us. "What are you working on?"

"A chalkboard sign that goes on the sidewalk," I told her.

"Fiona's relatives have that other bakery, and her aunt is making these really amazing cookies and stuff, but they aren't on the menu, so they need a sign like at the barbershop but better," Julia added. "Her great-uncle is an artist. He could probably do your sign for you."

Elfine was looking at me. "Amazing cookies, huh? Renee told me Becky was baking something new. And Tim's finally doing art again, too?"

"How do you know them?" I asked. It was weird having everybody know my relatives better than I did.

She laughed. "It's a small town. I went to school with Tim, and I taught shop class when Becky was in high school. Let's see. . . . Are you Sheila's daughter?"

I nodded and changed the subject before she could ask how my mom was doing and why I was here. "Did Great-Uncle Timothy—I mean, Tim, I guess—did he used to do a lot of art?"

"Tim was always drawing. I never saw him without a pen

or pencil in his hand, looking at his paper instead of at the rest of us."

I hesitated. I didn't want to talk behind people's backs. But it's okay to check and see what other people think when you're worried about someone. "Did he used to talk back then?" I really wasn't sure how to fix that, if it needed fixing. But maybe Ms. Davis would know.

She smiled. "Tim's always been quiet." She shrugged. "My friend Clarice decided that he had so much to say with his art, he didn't have anything left over to put into words."

"Then why doesn't he do more art?" I asked. "Why does he just work in the bakery?"

"When Tim and Robert finished school, everyone expected them to work at the bakery. Saying no to your family—well, that can be a hard thing to do. And after Robert died . . ." Elfine sighed. "I'm glad to hear he's finally picked up a pen again, though. Life's too short not to do what you were put on this earth for, and none of us are getting any younger."

Julia frowned at the marker. "How do they put chalk in pens? Do they work, or are they just a gimmick?"

"Try one for yourself," Elfine said. She handed Julia a blue chalk pen labeled SAMPLE and a clipboard that had been painted with chalkboard paint. "We've got regular chalk, too, and a kind that's more like crayons. But the markers are nice if you're doing something you don't want to smudge. You have to use a wet rag to get them off."

Julia drew a witch's hat with a moon and stars on the clipboard. It looked great, not smudged at all. Then she gave it to me, and I drew a magic wand.

"I think you should get these," Julia told me.

"I think I should get some, too. Can I borrow your paint if you have any left after you finish your sign? I bet my dad has a clipboard like this somewhere."

"Sure," I told her.

So we each bought a pack of chalk markers. I bought the chalkboard paint and a couple of paint rollers, too, and paper masks that go over your nose and mouth that Elfine said we had to use when painting.

"Tell Becky and Tim that Elfine Dumond says hi," she said.

I promised I would. She didn't say anything about Great-Aunt Alta. Neither did I.

"Can I help you paint the sign?" Julia asked as we unlocked our bikes.

"Sure, if we can find somewhere to paint it that won't

make a mess," I said. "You can take the leftover paint home afterward. That clipboard will be cool." I wished I had a clipboard around that I could paint. But maybe I could buy one after she gave the paint back.

Julia was watching me. "Want me to make you one, too?"

"Yes, please," I answered, smiling.

12

WHEN WE GOT to Aunt Becky's bakery, it was filled with the smell of warm coconut. I felt a little sick, and not just because I was full of the other bakery stuff.

Aunt Becky was concentrating on the mixer. She looked like she was lost in her recipe thoughts again, getting ready for her next attack.

"Portia says you should do yellow and red peppers for flames and olives for the hilts," Julia told her. "And you have to cut the mushrooms straight."

Aunt Becky just blinked.

"Elfine Dumond says hi," I told Great-Uncle Timothy—Tim, Elfine had called him. Yeah, he seemed more like a Tim. "Do you need a break?"

He shook his head.

"Then can we paint your sign in the parking lot?" I asked. "Or is there a better place to do it?"

He pulled his keys out of his pocket. First he held them up by the car key.

"Yeah, I know," I said. "It's in the trunk. Julia can help me get it out."

Then he held up another key. He pointed at the door to the hallway and handed me the keys.

I knew you couldn't paint in a closet, because you'd probably die of fumes. But maybe there were newspapers back there or something. You can't really express a complicated thought like that just by pointing. At least he tried. "Thanks," I told him, and went to see what was in the closet.

Julia followed right behind me. "Your great-uncle *really* doesn't talk much," she said as the hallway door closed behind her.

"I know." I shrugged. "But maybe he'll start talking through his art again. It's better than not at all, right? That reminds me—I have to tell you about his shed!" I put the key in the lock, turned it until it clicked, and opened the door.

It wasn't a closet. It was a tiny yard, with huge green plants everywhere.

"This is *amazing*," Julia said, her eyes shining.

It wasn't exactly beautiful, with the battered old building walls surrounding it. But with the jungly plants and the lost-garden vibe, it did seem perfect for a witch. I walked over to a gravel patch where the plants weren't as thick. It looked far enough from the fence and the buildings that I didn't think we'd get paint on anything we weren't supposed to. "Do you think paint hurts plants?"

"These are weeds," Julia said with great authority. "Dandelions and thistles and Scotch broom—nobody planted any of this. It's hard work to get rid of them."

She sounded like she knew her stuff, so I nodded. "Then let's do it."

Aunt Becky didn't look up when we came back in, but Great-Uncle Tim smiled when I gave him a thumbs-up. He watched as we carried the sign and the paint and everything through the back door.

I told Julia about Great-Uncle Tim's secret art shed while she helped me stomp down the weeds growing through the gravel. I told her it was a secret, and I knew she wouldn't tell, so I didn't think he'd mind.

Then I shook the paint can while Julia set up the sign. I wrangled the lid off the paint can. Julia put her mask on, pulled it up over her nose, and picked up her roller.

"Don't go too fast, or it will splatter," Julia said as I put my mask on, too. "I saw it on TV."

She rolled the paint on one side, and I started on the other, spreading the paint around so it covered the wood. It looked shiny, but Julia said that was just because it was still wet. When it was all as black as a chalkboard, I set my roller down, then took off the mask so the breeze could dry my sweaty chin and nose.

Julia took hers off, too. She waved her hand at the plants.

"Is this your great-aunt's witch garden? Is she going to lock us up in a tower if she catches us here?"

"I don't think so," I said. "We're not princesses, after all. As far as I know, she just stays home all day, unless she decides to go yell at someone."

"That's not very witchlike," Julia said. She put the lid back on the paint can and hit it with a rock until it stayed on. "Witches are supposed to get things done."

I nodded. "Like fairy godpeople."

"Kind of," Julia said. "Only, witches focus on their own goals, instead of other people's wishes. The whole good-witch, bad-witch thing . . ." She shrugged. "That's just whether other people like a witch's goal or not."

"It seems like she just wants everything to stay the same, always." I frowned. "And I don't think that makes her a good witch."

"It sounds really boring." Julia wiped the paint off her hands with some dandelion leaves. "Why would she stay home when she could be here? This place is great."

I thought about Great-Aunt Alta lurking around her creepy old house all day, with nothing to do except moan and groan about everything. "Maybe she needs a hobby. She was tapping a lot, so I thought maybe she wanted to be a spy. But I brought her some articles on how to get a spy job, and she just recycled them."

"What was she tapping?" Julia wanted to know. "Was it Morse code?"

"The same thing she always taps," I said. "Tap . . . tap . . . tap . . . tap-tap. Tap-tap-tap-tap-tap-tap . . ."

"Okay, let's look this up. Maybe it's a message!" Julia pulled out her phone. "I guess a tap and a pause is one dash? I don't really know how you separate letters and words and stuff if you don't have real beeps, just taps."

"Me either. But if we get the letters, maybe we can figure it out."

Julia nodded, not looking up. "One dash is a *t*. Dot-dot is an *i*. So, *t-t-t-i*? And then . . . how many taps after that?"

I tapped and counted again. "Uh . . . six?"

Julia frowned and put her phone away. "Five dots is the number five. But six dots doesn't mean anything."

I sighed. "So much for that idea. I guess she's just restless or something. Thanks anyway."

"You could still get her some library books," Julia suggested. "Like you did for your great-uncle."

"Yeah, but what kind of books?" I asked.

Julia shrugged. "Lots of different kinds. Maybe if she's bored, she'll pick one up and get interested."

"She wouldn't tell me if she did, though," I pointed out.

"Well, if she's not a spy, then I know a spy trick that should work on her!" Julia yanked a hair out of her head. "You put one hair between two pages of a book, like a bookmark. Then you check the book every day and see if it's still there. If it's gone, then someone opened the book."

I nodded, impressed. "How did you learn that?"

"Well, witches have to pretend to be harmless old ladies sometimes. So I got a spy book so I could learn how to do it."

Julia's phone rang. "Yeah, I know, Dad," she said. "I'm heading home in a minute. We've been busy." She hung up. "Can we hang out here again tomorrow?"

I smiled. "Sure. You should take one of Aunt Becky's new cookies, too. They're magic!"

KEVIN AT THE LIBRARY WAS VERY HELPFUL, EVEN THOUGH HE DIDN'T know if Great-Aunt Alta liked any kinds of books in particular, since he'd never seen her at the library. He didn't know if she had any friends I could ask, either.

"I only ever see her at the town festival," he admitted.

"Great-Aunt Alta goes to a festival? Like, for fun?" I stared at him.

He grinned. "The Cold Hope Festival is kind of a big deal here. It takes place in the park across the way, and the parade runs down Main Street. There's games and stuff, and every kind of fried food you can imagine. Becky never mentioned the baking contest?"

I shook my head slowly.

"There's a concert, too—Alta comes for that. She and Tim and Becky perform the same song every year."

I tried to picture any of them on a stage and couldn't. "What kind of song?"

"Also sprach Zarathustra," he said. "It's from a movie. Alta plays the drums."

Huh. "What drums?" I asked. "I've never seen any drums there." Although that could explain why she was always tapping her fingers. . . .

"Timpani, I think—big drums." He shrugged. "Maybe she puts them away when she's not practicing. I think we have a CD you can check out, if you want to hear it." He turned back to the computer.

I looked at the new-book shelf while he searched. Since there wasn't any way to know what Great-Aunt Alta would like, I picked out one book each about all kinds of things: art in museums, hockey, bird-watching, crocheting little foods with faces. . . .

"Got it," Kevin said, writing something down. He led me back to the music section, found the CD with Great-Aunt Alta's song, and handed it to me.

It was a movie soundtrack, with a space scene on the cover. "Do you have any books about space?" I asked. "And about music? I just need one of each for now."

While he looked them up, I flipped through the CDs, in case anything else looked good. I didn't know any of the bands, so I just picked CDs with interesting covers. One was mostly black, with a triangle and a rainbow; one had a yellow submarine on it that I remembered from a movie I watched with my mom when I was little; one had another space scene, with two planets really close together; and one had gloomy-looking people in black-and-white face paint. That one looked like her kind of vibe.

I THOUGHT ABOUT ASKING GREAT-AUNT ALTA ABOUT HER SONG THAT night while we were eating dinner. But I'd had a long day, and I wanted to try Julia's spy trick first anyway. Spies don't just ask people what they want to know, unless they've captured them first. So, after dinner and dishes, I went up to my room and got to work.

After some consideration, I decided there were too many books to yank out a hair for each one. That would hurt, and I didn't want to have a bald patch. Besides, I didn't want it to stick out both ends of the book. So I pulled a few out and cut them up into sections with my craft scissors. The CDs didn't have pages, so I just stuck a hair in each case. Then I made a note on the "Library Due Date" page of my notebook, so I'd remember to take all the hairs out before I turned them back in to the library.

I waited until I heard Great-Aunt Alta creak up the stairs and stomp off to her room. Then I carried all the books and CDs downstairs and spread them out on the coffee table so she couldn't miss them.

When that was done, I crept back up the stairs, avoiding the creaking parts, just like a spy. I got out my notebook and made a hair-checking log.

13

NOTHING HAD CHANGED when I inspected the hairs the next morning. But maybe Great-Aunt Alta hadn't seen what I'd brought home for her yet? I made a note to check again that night.

When we got to the bakery, I examined the sign. It felt dry and smooth, just like a chalkboard, with only a few little bumps and drips. I carried it inside and set it down in front of Great-Uncle Tim. Then I got the chalk markers out of my backpack and gave them to him. "These are for you."

He got a funny smile, like the one I've seen on his face when Renee delivers the mail. He didn't say thanks. But the way he clutched his new markers tight made me feel like he had.

My shoulders relaxed a little. Things with Aunt Becky and her friend might still be messed up. But what could go wrong with art?

I marched over to Aunt Becky, who was looking through her recipe box again. "What are we selling today?"

She looked up, confused, like she'd been thinking about something else.

"Great-Uncle Tim needs to write and draw it on our new chalkboard sign," I explained. "I don't know how to change your old sign, so we made a new one for the sidewalk. He can change it every day, if you want. He'll do the writing and the art."

Aunt Becky nodded. "Pistachio-oatmeal bars with raspberry jam. Blueberry bran muffins with ginger. Banana bread with chocolate chips. And a few other things. . . ."

So I started getting the muffin ingredients out while Aunt Becky and Great-Uncle Tim decided what went where on the new sign.

Then Aunt Becky started up the Enormous Mixer of Danger, and Great-Uncle Tim started writing on the sign. On one side he wrote "Baker's Favorites" and added the new muffins and banana bread and Aunt Becky's favorite cookies.

"And the magic cookie bars," I said. "Those are Julia's favorite. She helped us out, so she's practically a baker, too."

He nodded and added them. On the other side he wrote "Daily Specials" and added the coconut-lime cupcakes and the flaming-sword pizzas. He wrinkled his nose and sighed.

So did I. But what could we do?

And then he started drawing all around the words.

Before he started, it looked pretty much like the barbershop's sign. But once Great-Uncle Tim got going, it was like he couldn't stop. He filled in every bit of space with swirls and flowers and cool squiggles and those little lines that make something look like it's special and glowing in comic books.

And then, finally, he ran out of room. I watched him, to see if going back to his regular work made him sad after all that art.

But he looked up at me and smiled. And for the first time since I'd met him, he didn't look sad at all.

I made Aunt Becky come and admire it, too. We both told him how great it looked. Then I took the sign out front. I picked a spot where people could see it but wouldn't run into it, and stood back to admire it one more time. It was so nice to see something that had really gone right—at least, as long as I wasn't looking at the side with all Aunt Becky's battle stuff.

"That's *amazing*!" Julia said, rolling up on her bike.

"I know!" I said, grinning at her. "It's just like I planned it! Thanks for helping. I have to tell you about the stuff I checked out of the library for Great-Aunt Alta."

Julia got off her bike and locked it. "I brought you a clipboard. Let's try them out in your enchanted garden, and you can fill me in."

That sounded pretty great to me.

WE'D JUST FINISHED SOME MUFFINS AND WERE STARTING TO DRAW when Great-Uncle Tim stuck his head out the secret-garden door.

"Check it out!" Julia cried, showing him the broom she'd drawn on her clipboard.

He gave her an almost-smile. Then he looked at me, sighed, and tipped his head toward the inside of the bakery.

"Do you need help? Or is someone here or something?" I asked. I hoped it wasn't Great-Aunt Alta here yelling again.

Great-Uncle Tim shook his head, then nodded. I must have looked confused, because he gave up and held the door open.

Julia followed me inside.

Portia was there, standing in front of the bakery counter. On the counter was an open box. Inside the box was a big chocolate tart. And on top of the tart was a pirate ship, with

a skull-and-crossbones flag and everything. There were even tiny cannons on the deck.

Aunt Becky was staring down at it.

Portia was watching her, waiting.

"Hi, Portia!" Julia said cheerfully. "Look what I drew!"

"Hey, Jules," Portia said. She took a long, careful look at Julia's broom. Then she smiled and nodded. "Nice. I can tell from the sparks that's no ordinary broomstick."

Julia grinned. She waved her hand at the pirate ship. "Did you help Annie with this?"

"Nah, I'm just delivering it," Portia said. She looked at Great-Uncle Tim. "Did you do the sign out front?"

He looked nervous. But he nodded.

"I like it," she said seriously. "Elfine told me about some of the art you used to make. Your sculptures sounded cool. You should do something for the parade."

I watched Great-Uncle Tim's face light up when he heard her words and then sag into its usual sadness. Maybe my work there wasn't quite done.

Aunt Becky turned abruptly and opened a drawer. She pulled out a big knife.

"Whoa, there, Aunt Becky!" I said, stepping back.

But Julia had already figured out what she was up to. "Can I try a piece?" she asked as Aunt Becky hacked up the tart.

Aunt Becky nodded absently, even though it was way before lunch. She passed the knife to Portia, then took a bite, closing her eyes. Portia cut small slices for the rest of us, including herself. Aunt Becky opened her eyes suddenly, glared at the tart, and stalked over to the mixer.

I watched her, feeling uneasy. Was it time to speak my truth again? Already? I hadn't even told Ms. Davis about speaking my truth to Annie yet. Besides, Aunt Becky clearly was not in a listening mood.

"Is this stuff edible?" Julia asked, poking the chunk of ship perched on top of her slice with her fork.

"Yeah, but it doesn't taste good," Portia said. "It's fondant. It's kind of like if you made Play-Doh out of sugar."

Julia took a small bite of it anyway. She sighed and pushed it off her tart. "At least the tart tastes okay."

Renee came in after Portia left. "Hello, Fiona. Hello, Julia," she said. "Hello, Tim." She shouted over the noise of the mixer, "Hello, Becky!"

Aunt Becky didn't look up.

"I don't think she means to be rude," I told Renee. "She's just really focused right now."

" 'Focused,' " Renee said thoughtfully. "Yes, that's a good word for your family." She didn't look mad, though. "That sign is beautiful, Tim. It really brightened my day. It's a pity the post office doesn't have anything colorful like that." She sighed. "I'll take one each of today's specials."

I hesitated. Today's specials were Aunt Becky's battle foods—the coconut-lime cupcakes and the flaming-sword pizzas. (And maybe whatever else Aunt Becky was making, once she came back to this world from wherever her head was now.) If I gave Renee a cupcake, she might tell everyone in town.

This was definitely a situation I didn't feel good about.

"Do you want me to get them?" Julia asked.

Might as well get speaking my truth over with. "You can

buy a cupcake," I told Renee. "But you should know that they were supposed to be an apology. Aunt Becky didn't mean to start anything. At least, I hope she didn't."

Renee put her hands on her hips. "What on earth is happening now?"

I waited for the mixer to stop roaring through my thoughts and tried to think how to explain the situation.

Great-Uncle Tim started drawing on a paper bag. We all watched him. When he was done, he passed me the bag. It was the cupcake story in comic-book form.

I slid it across the counter to Renee. "This. Pretty much."

"Where did Kevin get a cape?" Julia asked, going around the counter to peer at the drawing.

"Not a cape," I said. "That's artistic . . . whatever. And we don't actually know what Aunt Becky's friend thought, because we weren't there."

Renee examined the rest of the tart, pirate flag still flying. "I see," she said slowly.

"Any tips?" I asked. You never know with dragons. Sometimes they're very wise.

"Do I just put what she wants in a bag?" Julia asked.

"We use a small box for cupcakes, so the frosting doesn't get smashed," I told her. "Wait—shower cap first!" I helped Julia put her special bakery shower cap on. I still wasn't sure if we had to wear them when we were helping people as well as when we were making cookies. But it wasn't a good time to ask Aunt Becky.

Renee looked up from the comic. "How are the cupcakes?" she asked as I handed her her change and the bakery box.

"Delicious," Julia said. "Annie's are super cute, but they don't taste as good."

Renee nodded. "Same old fight, then. Well, at least they can have it out now."

The chocolate tart still felt as heavy as an anchor in my stomach. "I just wanted to help," I told her. "But now she won't stop."

"Neither will Annie," Julia put in. "And Fiona doesn't like it when people fight."

Renee nodded thoughtfully. "Well, the festival baking competition is this Sunday—what about that? Winner takes all, and the battle ends there and then."

"Like a duel or something," Julia said. "You can't keep fighting after a duel is over. . . . It could work."

I didn't want them to fight at all. But I didn't have any better ideas. "Aunt Becky, can we talk to you for a minute?" I shouted over the mixer.

She shut it off and came to join us. "What is it?"

I took a deep breath, gathering up what I wanted to say, again. Speaking your truth isn't ever very easy. But that doesn't mean you don't have to do it. "I'm glad you aren't just baking your same old boring things every day," I told her. "But this bakery war is getting out of control. So we were wondering if you could just have a duel instead?"

"A *duel*?" Aunt Becky said, like she had no idea who she'd be fighting. As if.

"Yeah, at the festival's baking competition," Julia said.

"Unless you're not planning to take part?" Renee asked, watching Aunt Becky.

Slowly, Aunt Becky smiled. I could see that in her head she was cackling just like Annie had. "Oh, I'll be there." She turned and strode back to her recipe box, like she wasn't even seeing us anymore.

14

"YES, THEY'D BETTER have it out," Renee said, grinning. "Tim, you can help her with a letter challenging Annie, and I'll pick it up and deliver it tomorrow."

I watched as Renee strode out the door.

"Your sign really is beautiful," Julia told Great-Uncle Tim.

He kind of smiled at her, but he didn't really look happy. Actually, he looked not just unhappy but pretty uncomfortable. Maybe he didn't like it when people fought, either. Or maybe he had to go to the bathroom or something. "Do you want to take a break?" I asked him. "I can help the customers for a little while."

He hesitated for a moment.

"And I can help Fiona," Julia offered.

Great-Uncle Tim stared at his shoes and nodded. Then he walked slowly back through the door that led to the hallway with the secret garden (and the bathroom).

"What are you making now?" Julia asked Aunt Becky. "Is that black food coloring?"

"Cannonball frosting," Aunt Becky said, smiling grimly. "For the coconut-lime cupcakes."

I sighed. "What happened to making your favorite recipes?"

"Plenty of time for that after I win," she said, revving up the mixer.

So Julia and I helped customers while Aunt Becky mixed food coloring into her cream-cheese frosting until it was a weird gray color. She plopped a whole lot of it onto each of the cupcakes, mounding it up so it looked like a ball that had been cut in half.

"I'm not so sure people are going to want to eat those," I told her.

But she was looking around, not listening. "Where's Uncle Timothy? He needs to change the sign."

He had been gone kind of a while. "Be right back,"

I told her. The bathroom was empty, so I grabbed Julia's hand and pulled her toward the secret garden with me.

"I don't think he likes this. Aunt Becky isn't really being her best self right now," I whispered as I opened the door. We stepped outside, and I fell silent.

Great-Uncle Tim was drawing on the walls of the buildings all around the garden in chalk. Not just little tiny stuff, but huge trees, and flowers almost as big as the trees, and clouds up as high as he could reach. It felt like he'd drawn a way out of our secret garden full of weeds and into an enchanted forest.

"Wow," Julia said softly.

But not so softly that he didn't hear. He gave a start and stopped drawing, his hand dropping down to hang by his side, like when someone stops moving one of those puppets on strings. He didn't look at us.

"This is incredible!" I told him honestly. I didn't think

you were really supposed to draw on other people's buildings without asking them, even in chalk. But he was the adult here, and if he wasn't worried about it, I wasn't going to bring it up.

"It's like Banksy," Julia said.

Great-Uncle Tim turned. He stared at her, then at his chalk art and back again. Slowly, one of his eyebrows went up.

"What's Banksy?" I asked.

"This anonymous street artist," Julia said. "No one knows who they are or anything about them."

"What's street art?" I asked. "People drawing on the street? Like hopscotch? Or art that you can drive, like cars covered with stuff or floats in a parade?"

"Nah, it's art that's on buildings and sidewalks and stuff," Julia said. "Although a float would be cool, too! Banksy just appears and makes really cool art, out where everyone can see it. Then they disappear again. Art that says something about life and asks questions and makes you think. Art that changes how you see the world. Sometimes it's hidden in plain sight, where no one expects there to be any art—like on city streets. Or sometimes Banksy turns up in disguise in a museum and does something there. The museums get pretty excited when that happens." She shrugged. "You can probably find out more at the library."

Maybe, when I had time. But first I had some things to

do. "When you're done with your break, Aunt Becky would like you to change 'cupcakes' to 'cannonball cupcakes' on the sign," I told Great-Uncle Tim.

He didn't say no. He didn't even shake his head. But he didn't look very happy.

I know how it feels to be caught in the middle of something when you don't want to be. I tried to remember what Ms. Davis had told me some of the times when I felt that way. "Just because someone else is having a bad day—or a bad idea—doesn't mean it has to wreck your day, too," I said. "So I think you should keep drawing what makes you happy until you're ready to come in. I can help Aunt Becky until then. Maybe she'll rethink her plan if she has to wait awhile." I looked up at his chalk forest and smiled.

"I wish the whole town could be covered in art like this!" Julia said. Her eyes were shining.

Great-Uncle Tim stared at her for a minute. Then he smiled. It was a small smile. But a real one.

IT WAS A GOOD THING WE GOT BACK INSIDE WHEN WE DID. AUNT BECKY was headed for the front door, totally ignoring the customers lining up. (Honestly, no wonder the bakery had problems before I got here.) She was holding a piece of chalk and a paper towel.

"Uh-uh," I said firmly, hurrying between her and the door. "Great-Uncle Tim worked hard on that sign. You can't just go changing it without asking him first. When he's done with his break, you can talk to him about it."

"But I need to—" Aunt Becky went for the door.

"Nope," I told her, folding my arms. "His art is important to him. You should respect that. You remember what it felt like when you finally got to make your cookies, don't you? He doesn't go around dumping stuff in your recipes when you're not looking, and you wouldn't like it if he did. So don't act like your work is more important than his."

Aunt Becky was staring at me, her mouth hanging open a little. She blinked.

"Yeah, just like Fiona said," Julia said, nodding. She went up to the first person in line. "What can we get for you?"

I don't know how long it was before Great-Uncle Tim came inside. But when Aunt Becky asked him to change the sign for her, he did—although I noticed he didn't change his art around the words or start drawing a lot of cannons or anything.

"Can we go draw now?" Julia asked.

Great-Uncle Tim came back up to the register.

"Are you okay for a while?" I asked him.

He still didn't look as happy as he had earlier, but he nodded.

So I led the way back into the garden. "Thanks for helping us out," I said. "Aunt Becky's not very good with words. But she probably appreciates your help, too."

"She's good at baking, though!" Julia said. She stared up at Great-Uncle Tim's magic chalk garden. "Just like he's really good at art."

It was true. He'd added an awesome dragon in a whole rainbow of colors.

Julia grinned. "Look, he signed it!"

I looked all over and finally found his signature under a huge leaf.

He'd signed it "Bakesy."

After lunch, we went to the library so Julia could get some of the books I thought she'd like and I could check my email and meet with Mr. Rivera.

Dearest Fiona,

I meant to email you yesterday, but I had so much to do here that I couldn't. I keep telling them I already know this stuff, but they don't listen—they say I have to do it anyway. I can't wait to be done with this place.

I miss you so much.

Love,
Mom

Dear Mom,

It's okay, Mom. I know you have more important stuff to do than email me. It sounds kind of like school. You know—you have to do the stuff they tell you, even if you already know it, or you get a bad grade. My teacher says it's good practice anyway. Maybe if you get it done fast, you'll have time to hang out with your friends there.

My friend Julia taught me how to paint a sign. It turned out great! Great-Uncle Tim drew cool stuff on it.

I am fine. I miss you.

Love,
Fiona

Dear Ms. Davis,

You were right. Helping people isn't as easy as it looks. I mean, it could be—I've had some great ideas for how to make things better. Sometimes my relatives even try them. But everything goes wrong, somehow. No matter how many times I speak my truths.

1. *I spoke my truth to Aunt Becky's frenemy, about how the cupcakes were my idea and were supposed to be an apology. You know what she did? She cackled!*
2. *I spoke my truth to Aunt Becky, about not messing with Great-Uncle Tim's art, even though she wanted to change something. But she should have known that on her own.*
3. *I spoke my truth to Renee, about how I didn't mean to start a war, so not to tell everyone I did.*

Oh, and I guess I spoke a little of my truth to my friend Julia, and her friend Portia. But that was just about my feelings. And I told Great-Uncle Tim some of the things you tell me when someone has a bad day. But those are really your truths.

I'm trying to focus on the positives. Aunt Becky is still

baking stuff she's interested in. Great-Aunt Alta doesn't really tell her not to anymore, so I guess she got over her issues, or at least she's keeping them to herself. But if Aunt Becky is still trying to be friends instead of frenemies again, she's doing it wrong. She's spending all her time on a recipe for a baking duel, and she's focused on winning, not apologizing. Honestly, at this point I'm not even sure I should keep trying to help her. But who else will?

At least Great-Uncle Tim is doing more of his art. He draws on the bakery boxes and bags sometimes, in between ringing up customers. And he really went all out on the chalkboard sign we made.

I haven't forgotten about Great-Aunt Alta, either. I checked some stuff out from the library for her, in case she's bored. She's always talking about everything that's wrong, but it's never very specific. I mean, when you ask someone how their day was and they tell you life is full of suffering, how do you fix that?

I am still fine. (Just kidding.) Mr. Rivera isn't the same as you, but he's pretty good. We checked in again today. He wanted to talk about how I'm doing, and about my mom. I miss her a lot. But I know there's nothing I can do to help her right now. All I can do is learn how to help people better—not just better, but as good as you. That way I'll never mess up. That way, when she has problems, she'll need me there with her. I never want to be sent away again.

I didn't really want to talk about that much, though. So Mr. Rivera and I talked about my lessons instead. He told me he tries to remember that everyone has their own story to live—even fairy godpeople. We can watch other people's stories unfold, we can tell them what we're seeing, and we can try to help them as best we can. But we can't write their stories for them. And if they're doing things we don't think are good for them and that we don't want to be part of, we can speak our truths and tell them that. We can even stop helping them. Even when things might get messy without our help. Because if we don't say what we're really thinking, our stories will just fill up with things like "One day Fiona helped her aunt bake a Trojan horse out of gingerbread, although she secretly thought it was a terrible idea."

But he doesn't know everything. So I'm still trying.

Your apprentice,
Fiona

P.S. I need my next lesson now, please.

15

WHEN WE PULLED up to Great-Aunt Alta's house that afternoon and got out of the car, I thought I heard something, just for a moment. Like someone screeching or crashing around. But it cut off suddenly as we walked up the path. And when we got inside, Great-Aunt Alta was sitting in her chair like she always is, tapping away on the arm.

That night, after we ate our silent dinner in the gloomy old dining room, Aunt Becky wrote her letter challenging Annie to a baking duel while I read a couple chapters of that witch book Julia picked out for me. (Julia was right—it's *so good*!) Then Great-Uncle Tim and I went to his art shed so he could make the letter look right for an important duel invitation. He let me crunch it up into a ball and dip it into a cup of tea. When it was dry, he rolled it up and melted part of an old candle onto it to seal it shut, and stuck a fork in the hot wax to make a fancy *B*, for "Becky." He didn't look happy about it, though, even if it was kind of like art.

I wasn't so sure a duel would fix everything, either. I tried to think of a backup plan while I brushed my teeth and got ready for bed. But how could I make someone apologize or make things better when she didn't seem to want to anymore? I couldn't concentrate on the book I was reading at all. And when I stopped trying and turned out the light, I found myself missing my mom so much, I couldn't sleep.

I had to check the hairs in the books and CDs anyway. So I crept out of my room, into the dark hallway, and down the stairs, being careful not to crash into anything and wake everyone up.

The hairs were still in most of the books and the CDs. But the one in the music encyclopedia was missing. So was the one in the CD with Great-Aunt Alta's song and the one with the black-and-white face paint.

When I was done, I crept back up the stairs and curled up on the padded bench in the big window overlooking the street. I stared out into the night. What if the people who were trying to help my mom break her curse weren't doing it right? What if no one could help her? The old house creaked and groaned around me. It didn't help my mood.

Then one creak sounded louder than the rest, somewhere downstairs. I froze. Was it Great-Aunt Alta, creeping around in the dark like a vampire? It seemed like her style. But then the creak was followed by a click. Then nothing.

At least, not until I heard the sound of a car door

opening. I peered through the window. Someone was climbing into the big old car we drove to the bakery every morning.

The car wasn't being stolen, though. It was Great-Uncle Tim, dressed all in black, with a black knitted hat over his white hair, even though it was summer and not cold at all. He started up the engine.

As I watched him drive slowly away, I wondered what had gone wrong this time.

THE NEXT MORNING, RENEE CAME IN WITH NEWS AS WELL AS OUR mail. Aunt Becky was busy doing something secret with the Enormous Mixer of Danger, and Great-Uncle Tim was doing new art for today's sign, so Renee gave me the mail.

"You'll never guess what's happened now," Renee said, watching Great-Uncle Tim draw.

"What?" I asked, hoping it didn't have anything to do with Great-Uncle Tim sneaking out. What if he'd lost a shoe somewhere?

"Clarice Cosgrove broke her ankle!" Renee said.

Well, that wasn't what I had expected.

"You might not have met Clarice yet. She works up at the town hall," Renee said. "She's in charge of all the official Cold Hope business . . . including the festival! You know, the one with the baking competition? Where Becky and Annie will duel?" Renee sighed and turned back to Great-Uncle Tim. "You haven't told her anything about the festival?"

He glanced up at her. His cheeks got red, and he gave her a funny little smile, then looked away again without answering.

Renee rolled her eyes. But I noticed she had a funny little smile, too.

"Kevin told me about the festival," I said. "But what has that got to do with a broken ankle?"

"Right! Well, you might need a new plan for Becky's duel, since the festival may not even happen now."

That got Great-Uncle Tim's attention. Even Aunt Becky frowned and turned off the mixer. "It's the day after tomorrow," she said. "They can't just cancel it."

"Who'll run everything, though?" Renee said. "Dr. Mudel said Clarice has to stay in bed and absolutely immobile until her surgery. Her son says he'll only run her errands and all that if she does what the doctor tells her to. So she's stuck." She sighed. "Such a pity. She'd gotten everything almost done, of course—Clarice is very organized. But someone has to be at the festival to manage the baking competition and the parade and the evening concert. . . . There are just too many pieces, and Clarice can't do it all by email."

"Maybe she's got a friend she can ask," I said.

Renee shook her head. "We talked it all over—I was the one who took her to the hospital, since it happened right outside the post office this morning. There aren't a lot of people around that early."

Out of the corner of my eye, I saw Great-Uncle Tim freeze. I tried not to look at him, but I had a bad feeling. "What happened?" I asked, trying to sound casual.

"That's the strangest part!" Renee said. "Clarice told me she was out for her morning constitutional—she goes for a walk every day before work, rain or shine—and when she got to the post office, she saw that someone had spray-painted an enormous bouquet of flowers with a dragon curled around them on the wall. She was so surprised, she stepped right off the sidewalk without even seeing the curb and landed all wrong on her ankle. 'Done in by art,' she said." She leaned closer. "I'd come in the back, so I hadn't seen it yet—I just saw her go down. Good thing I happened to glance out the window when I did."

I tore my eyes away from Great-Uncle Tim, who was carefully turning the flower he'd been drawing into a butterfly.

"It's awfully pretty, though—much better than that boring blank wall. Flowers in every color of the rainbow. . . ." She sighed and looked out at the gray sky. "But enough with the news." She walked over and peered at the sign.

I held my breath. If Great-Aunt Alta yelled at Aunt Becky for making new cookies, she was *really* going to lose it if she found out her brother was breaking people's ankles with his art.

"I'll go with the blueberry bran muffin today," Renee said. "And a cup of coffee."

Phew. I got her muffin while Great-Uncle Tim got her coffee.

"If someone needed to talk to Clarice, how would they reach her?" I asked, trying to be casual. "Like, uh, maybe to tell her to get well soon or if they wanted to help out or something?"

Renee didn't look like she thought this was a weird question, even though it had sounded kind of strange coming out of my mouth. "She's on email," she said. "Same address she's always had—they can look it up at the library, if they don't already know it."

"Thanks," I told her, and gave her her change.

As soon as she left, I called Julia and asked her to meet me at the library.

Dearest Fiona,

Sweetie, there's no point making friends here. Not when I'll be gone any day. Yes, good news! I've learned everything I can here. And why would I stay when you need me? As soon as I figure out the details, I'll come get you.

I miss you so much.

Love,
Mom

I took a long breath in and held it. Then I let it go. It was great that Mom was learning fast, wasn't it? And I still wanted to go home. So why did my stomach feel like I'd swallowed an actual cannonball? Maybe because I had just moved here? Thinking about packing everything up again felt like those fair rides that whip your seat around, first one direction, then another, without letting your stomach catch up.

Or maybe because I remembered what Ms. Davis had said about how long she thought it would take. Mom's been too optimistic before. It didn't work out well.

Dear Mom,

I miss you, too. But your program goes all summer, and this is only the first week. Can't you give it a little longer? Maybe it's like when I thought I didn't like my fifth-grade teacher. She turned out fine once I got used to her style. Maybe this will, too.

You promised me you'd try this.

You promised, Mom.

Just stay there and keep learning until it's time to go home, okay?

Love,
Fiona

I tried to tell the cannonball in my stomach to turn back into one of Aunt Becky's cupcakes. I took another breath, held it, then let it out as slowly as I could. Then I moved on to Ms. Davis's email.

Dear Fiona,

You know, there's a big part of this work that we've never really talked about. That's learning how to keep yourself going. Even when things don't go the way you wanted.

Even when people won't let you help them. Sometimes it's just not the right time.

If you want to be ready when they finally decide to take that step forward, you have to practice helping yourself, too.

I think you're ready for your next lesson. It's time to try out your skills on yourself and see what you learn from the other side. It might be hard for you to focus on yourself, for once, instead of helping other people. But I know you can do it.

FAIRY-GODPERSON TRAINING: LESSON 3

1. Figure out something you want to do. Something for you, not for anybody else.
2. Make a plan to help yourself do it. Tell a buddy or a helper about your plan. Ask them to cheer you on and keep you accountable, so you'll actually do it. It's easy to shove your own plan aside to help someone else if no one's there to remind you.
3. Put your plan into action. Think about what works, and what could work better. What's harder than you expected? What's easier?

You can use what you learn when you help others. Where do you think that person might get stuck? Maybe someone could cheer them on, too.

There's something else I want you to know, Fiona. Even after all my years of doing this work, I can't help everyone. I don't always know what to do. Things still go wrong, usually in ways I never anticipated. All I can do is observe what's going on, speak my truths, and help myself, too, so I'm ready when they have a goal I can support. I'm not asking you to do anything that I don't have to do myself.

Sincerely,
Nia Davis

P.S. You're doing great.

P.P.S. I'll be off email until Monday. You can reply when-ever you want to, but I might not get back to you right away. Don't forget you can always call Mr. Rivera if you need something before then.

P.P.P.S. Don't forget to email your mom and tell her you love her. I know this has been hard for you. But I truly believe those words are better out than in.

Dear Ms. Davis,

My mom said she's done learning. She wants to make a plan and come get me. You know how you always say to pay attention to what my stomach thinks, because sometimes it has something important to tell me? Well, my stomach isn't happy about it.

I told her my truth—kind of. I said she should give it a little longer. I don't know if she'll listen, though. And of course I told her I love her. Just because I've got mixed-up feelings doesn't mean I don't love her. But I didn't tell her that my stomach feels scared. What if she does come to get me and we go home—and I can't help her?

I really thought I could, before. But now I don't know. I can't even help my relatives with their problems without stuff going wrong. And honestly, their problems are silly compared to hers.

Maybe wanting to help isn't enough. Maybe it will be like you said, and even experts like the people at her program won't be able to help her. Maybe her curse is just too powerful. Or maybe she won't let them help.

I don't know what to do. I guess I might as well practice on myself for a while, like you said. My friend Julia will probably help me.

I really am trying, Ms. Davis. But I'm getting pretty

tired of things not working out like they're supposed to. How come every fairy godperson in every story can wave their wand and get a happily-ever-after, but I can't even get a happily-for-now?

Your apprentice-fairy-godperson-in-training,
Fiona

P.S. Great-Uncle Tim snuck out last night. I know— Cinderella's fairy godmother helped her sneak out. But Cinderella wasn't drawing on buildings without asking permission first, or breaking people's ankles with her art. (By accident, not on purpose.) He's got a secret artist code name, so maybe no one will know it's him. But I'm still worried.

P.P.S. Maybe you feel like you aren't always that good at helping people, either. But you're still way better at it than I am.

P.P.P.S. Thanks for helping me all those times. I didn't know it was this hard.

16

JULIA GOT TO the library right after I finished my email to Ms. Davis. We went into the kids' section, and she flopped down on one of the beanbag chairs. "What's up? Did your great-aunt turn someone into a frog? Will she teach me how to do it?"

"Not yet." I set my backpack down and let myself topple over into the other beanbag. I lay there for a minute, trying to think how to even start.

"Is this about that dragon on the post office? Did your great-uncle do that?" Julia asked. "Do we need to break him out of jail or something?"

"How do you know about that? Did Renee tell you? Did she say it was Great-Uncle Tim?" This wasn't good.

"Nah, my aunt works across the street, so she told Dad about the art, and he told me. Nobody said anything about your great-uncle, and I didn't tell them he'd been drawing on buildings." Julia looked at me. I must have looked anxious, because she smiled. "I won't tell. So what do we do?"

"I don't think anyone else knows," I told her. "But Renee says Clarice broke her ankle and the festival will be canceled, and it might be Great-Uncle Tim's fault. . . ." I filled her in on all that. "I don't know how everything got so messed up. I thought I was doing okay with my lessons. But now Ms. Davis says I have to practice helping myself for a while. She was nice about it, but maybe I'm just making things worse." I showed her the email I'd printed out.

Julia read it carefully. "This doesn't say you screwed up. It says you have to do something *you* want to do. I can be your helper, no problem." She looked up at me. "So what do you want to do?"

"Save the festival," I told her.

"Okay, but why? For your aunt, so she can have her duel? Or for you?" Julia smiled. "Saving the festival isn't the fun part. It's the rest that's fun. Come on—it's not like having fun is hard."

Easy for her to say. There were so many things piled up in my mind that needed fixing—like a whole stack of cannonballs. How was I supposed to concentrate on anything else? "We can worry about that later."

"Nope." Julia shook her head. "It says I have to keep you accountable. That means you have to pick something fun and tell me. And then I have to make sure you do it."

I wasn't in the mood at all. But I took a breath and reminded myself that none of this was Julia's fault. "Fine. I want to go to the festival. The first step is saving it. Can we focus on that, please?"

"I'm going to write this down," Julia said. " 'Fiona wants to go to the festival'—and have fun, right? Not help your aunt with her duel or work there or whatever."

"I guess," I said.

Julia wrote it down in her notebook. Then she dug around in her backpack and handed me a red pen. "You ought to sign it in blood so it's official, but Kevin probably doesn't want you bleeding on his books, and I don't want to get kicked out of the library. So pretend this pen is full of your blood."

She folded her arms and waited while I signed her notebook page and wrote the date. "Okay," she said, putting the notebook away again. "Let's go see Clarice and figure out how we can help. I don't want the festival to get canceled, either. I want to watch the parade."

Finally. "We could bring her something from the bakery," I said. "As a get-well present."

I didn't know what Clarice would like. Neither did Julia. But when we went back to the bakery and I told Aunt Becky and Great-Uncle Tim we were going to see Clarice, Aunt

Becky put a big box of muffins and cookies and other stuff together, and Great-Uncle Tim drew her a get-well card and made her a cup of coffee with two sugars and one splash of cream. I hadn't known they even knew Clarice.

Julia studied the card. I kept an eye on her, in case she decided to ask him what he was up to. If he answered, I wanted to know, too.

But she didn't. "I like your art," she told him.

He smiled at her, a little sadly.

I checked the card for flowers and dragons. I didn't want Clarice to be reminded of her accident. And I really didn't want her to suspect Great-Uncle Tim of accidentally breaking her ankle. Not when he was finally doing his art where people could see it. (Even though we were going to have to talk about what he was up to later.) But he'd only drawn butterflies. We all signed it.

CLARICE LIVED IN AN APARTMENT NEAR THE LIBRARY. JULIA KNEW which number and everything. When we got there, Elfine from the hardware store was drilling holes in Clarice's front door. She put her drill down and smiled. "Here for Clarice?"

I nodded.

Elfine cracked the door open. "Julia and her friend Fiona are here to see you!"

"Send them in!" Clarice yelled back. She did not sound like a fragile old lady.

Elfine held the door open for us, and we went inside. No one was in the living room.

"Through the door to your right!" Clarice yelled again. "Don't trip over Reuben—he's around here somewhere."

At this, a big tabby stalked out of the kitchen and wove his way around our ankles.

"Hey, Reuben," Julia said, scratching him on the head.

Reuben licked her hand and butted it with his head. Then he led us through the door to our right.

Clarice looked to be about Elfine's age. She was sitting on a big bed with a wooden headboard. Carved lines radiated out all around her, making it look more like a throne than a bed. Her foot rested on another pile of pillows. Her pants leg was rolled up above her bare foot, and her ankle looked puffy and pink. I could see that her toenails were painted a sparkly purple. I wondered if she'd done that before she'd broken her ankle or after. Either way, it suited her.

"Thank you for coming," she said, like she'd asked us to, instead of us just showing up. She held out her hand. Julia put the coffee cup into it. Clarice took a sip, winced, and sighed. Then she smiled. "I know it's been a day when even Tim's dreadful coffee is a blessing. Julia, we'll need plates and napkins—you'll find them in the kitchen. We'll eat first, then discuss matters."

"We're here about the festival," I told her as Julia went off to find stuff. "We want to help."

"I thought as much," Clarice said. She patted the bed

beside her. Reuben jumped up. He kneaded the blanket for a moment, purring like a car engine. Then he curled up and went to sleep.

Clarice kept petting him anyway. Her face relaxed a little as she did it. "Julia is not a person who wastes time wringing her hands," she added as Julia returned with the plates and napkins. "And I'm guessing neither are you."

I put the blueberry bran muffins on the plates, since it was too early for cookies or cupcakes. "Not when something needs to get done."

Elfine leaned through the doorway. "The intercom's installed and ready to test," she said, handing Clarice a white box with two buttons.

Clarice nodded, and Elfine disappeared again. Clarice cleared her throat and pushed one of the buttons. "Who's there?" she asked. She let the button go.

"Testing . . . testing . . . ," Elfine's voice came back, a little staticky.

"Loud and clear," Clarice answered.

"Right. I'll get to work on the rest, then," Elfine said.

"Roger that," Clarice replied. She set the box on her bedside table. "Where were we?"

"Renee says someone has to be on the ground to make the festival happen," I told her.

"Exactly," Clarice said, putting her coffee down. "Now, here's what I need you to do. Go over to the hospital after four p.m. That's when Seth starts his shift. Go to emergency

admissions and ask to speak with him. Tell him I need to borrow one of their wheelchairs, just for a couple of weeks. Julia, I know they fit perfectly well in the back of your dad's car, so have him pick you up."

"But what about the festival?" I asked.

"That's where you two come in," Clarice said. "It's a pity you're not taller. But if one of you pushes the chair and the other keeps an eye out for obstacles, we should manage. You'll have to push fast if I'm to get from the bakery competition to the parade in time, though."

Julia was shaking her head. "No."

"What do you mean, 'no'?" Clarice asked, her eyes narrowing.

"Renee told Fiona that Dr. Mudel said you had to stay in bed until after your surgery," Julia said, folding her arms. "When Dr. Mudel tells you something, you're supposed to pay attention and do what she says."

Clarice sniffed. "What does she know about this?"

"Well, she *is* the doctor, right?" I said, folding my arms, too.

Julia nodded. "You know she and my dad are friends. He's not going to help us steal any wheelchairs behind her back. And you know she comes to the festival, too—what were you going to tell her when she caught you rolling around there?"

"I'd tell her, 'Told you I could do it!'" Clarice said.

But I knew that was just what Ms. Davis calls "huffing

and puffing," not useful talk at all. "I'd like to make a suggestion."

Clarice studied me. "Very well."

"Why don't you focus on taking care of yourself and *also* make a backup plan?" I said. "If you do what you're supposed to, maybe the doctor will decide your ankle is doing better and she'll let you go to the festival."

"That doctor can tell anyone whatever she thinks. And people just have to listen to her!" Clarice said. Which, I suspected, was the part that really bothered her.

"Yeah, she says most of her job is telling people stuff they don't want to hear," Julia said cheerfully. "So it's a good thing she's good at it. I vote yes for Fiona's plan." She stuck the rest of her muffin in her mouth.

"Julia and I can help you figure out the backup plan," I went on. "Maybe you won't even need it. But that way everyone will know the festival will still happen."

Clarice frowned. "I think you'd better go talk to Seth this afternoon."

Julia shook her head and swallowed. "Seth would probably do it for you," she said. "But then he'd get in trouble. You don't want that, do you?" She held Clarice's eyes until Clarice shook her head. "Good. Now, I think you need to listen to Fiona."

"Very well," Clarice said grumpily. "What have you got in mind?" She sounded like whatever it was, it was probably a bad idea.

"I think you need an apprentice," I told her. "Or maybe an heir." By now I was pretty sure who Clarice would be in a fairy tale.

"Why? I'm not going anywhere!" Clarice folded her arms.

"Neither is my fairy godmother, Ms. Davis—she's way too young to retire. But she took me on as her apprentice-fairy-godperson anyway," I told her. "She didn't exactly want to—she said no lots of times first."

"Then why did she agree?" Clarice asked, forgetting to be grumpy. (That happens when you tell someone something interesting.)

I shrugged. I didn't really want to get into my own stuff with her right then. "Ms. Davis says nobody's so important that the world can't run without them. And that it's not fair to make things better for people without finding a way to keep it going when you move on to something else."

"She sounds like a wise lady," Elfine said from the doorway. "I'd like to meet her someday."

"Maybe. She's pretty busy." I gave Clarice a look. "But she's still not too busy to take on an apprentice and teach someone else what she knows."

Clarice sighed. "I suppose she could have a point," she said, grumpy again.

But I could see that it wasn't so much that Clarice was mad at me as that she was mad at the situation she found herself in.

That was fine. Anyone with the energy to be grumpy has enough energy to get stuff done.

"Which of you wants to be my apprentice?" Clarice asked. "Or do I have to teach you both?"

Julia and I exchanged a look. "I'm going to be a witch, not a queen," Julia said. "And Fiona's going to be a fairy godperson, like she said. We can help you find other people and get started, though." She smiled at Clarice's frowny face. "What we need is a list!"

Clarice sighed again, but she picked up a notepad and pen from her bedside table.

"Renee said someone has to manage the baking competition, the parade, and the evening concert," I said. "Anything else?"

"Registration," Clarice said firmly, and wrote it down.

"The registration team has been managing perfectly well for years, and you know it," Elfine said, sitting down on the edge of Clarice's bed. "You've already got them signed up, right?"

"They always have questions, though," Clarice said. "Who will answer them if I'm not there?"

"Kevin," Elfine and Julia said immediately, together.

Clarice blinked.

"He already answers all the questions people have when you're not standing right there," Elfine told her.

"Besides, he's a librarian," Julia added. "He knows how to answer questions."

Clarice thought about it for a moment. I could see this stuff was important to her—she couldn't just let someone do a bad job of it. Not if she could help it.

Then, slowly, she nodded. "Kevin will do," she announced. "He'd better have a position title so everyone knows to direct their questions to him. 'Committee chair,' perhaps? Or 'team leader'?" She made some notes. Now that we were getting some work done, she looked a little happier. "Moving on, then—the baking competition."

"Not Aunt Becky or Annie," I said immediately. "They're going to have a duel—a baking duel."

"Lord, no!" Clarice said. "I'm certainly not putting either of them in charge. Who do we know who can manage both of them and everyone else who enters?"

We all thought hard. I knew Ms. Davis could deal with a couple of dueling bakers, no problem. But she wasn't here. That made me think, though. . . . "Mr. Rivera could do it."

Clarice's eyebrows rose. "An interesting choice," she said thoughtfully. "What do you think, Julia?"

"Sure, he could do it," Julia said. "He's a good eater. He hates coconut, but he'd be fair about it. And he deals with people who are mad about stuff all the time."

Clarice nodded. She wrote Mr. Rivera's name down.

"I have some thoughts about the parade," Julia announced.

"You may proceed," Clarice said, like we were at court or in a fancy meeting or something.

Julia went right ahead and proceeded. "Renee's going to be the announcer, like she always is, right?"

"Yes, of course," Clarice said, writing Renee's name down next to "Parade" and putting a ring of stars around it. "But she has to stay with the microphone at the announcer's stand—she can't solve the problems along the parade route, too."

"Right," Julia said. "But she can also be in charge of telling people where they have to be and when, since she has the microphone. So the other person just has to sort out traffic jams and people throwing candy too violently and things that fall off floats and whatever."

"Are you volunteering?" Clarice asked.

"No, I'm going to be busy making sure Fiona has fun, like she's supposed to," Julia said. "That might be a full-time job. So you should ask Portia."

"Portia?" Clarice asked blankly.

But I was nodding—she's the blacksmith, after all.

Elfine grinned. "You know—Mary's girl, with the colorful hair. She's home from college for the summer. Portia's perfect, if she's willing to do it. That girl gets things done, and she's no-nonsense about art. People will listen to her, even though she's new. I can talk to her, if you want."

Clarice didn't look so sure. But all she said was "I trust your judgment." She wrote Portia's name down next to Renee's, just as big, and gave her some stars, too.

"That leaves the concert, right?" Julia said.

"Well, there are other teams I supervise. . . ." Clarice trailed off and sighed as Elfine shook her head. "I suppose they already know their jobs perfectly well, though. I'll think on it. But yes, there must be someone to make announcements at the concert."

We all thought. Then we thought some more.

"I'll do it," Elfine said finally. "But I'm going to find someone to train as your backup for next year. I have other things to do, you know."

"I do know," Clarice said. "And I appreciate it. Thank you." She nodded at me and Julia. "Thank you girls, too." She looked funny for a moment, not funny-funny but sad-funny. Maybe she'd finally realized she might not be able to go this year.

"No problem," Julia said. "If that's all, we'd better go fill Renee in so she'll stop telling everyone it's not happening. Then we can see if Fiona's aunt is doing anything she'll regret today."

"I'll handle Renee," Clarice said. "You'd better go check on Becky." She peeked in the bakery box again and gave a shudder. "Swords on my pizza, indeed!"

Elfine peered in the box. "They'd look better with red and yellow peppers."

I sighed. "That's what Portia said. Julia told Aunt Becky, but she isn't really in a listening frame of mind, these days."

Elfine grinned. "Well, if Becky made them, at least they'll taste great."

There was one last thing I wanted to say, but I wasn't sure how. Since it was important, I just let the words come out anyway. "Clarice . . . I bet—I mean, I don't know, because how could I know?—but I bet whoever did that art wasn't trying to break your ankle. Maybe they just like art. A lot." I kept my eyes on Clarice's cat, still curled up, sound asleep. I wished I could pet him, but I didn't want to interrupt my important words to ask if it was okay.

"I should think not! Anyone who wanted to break my ankle would have much better results with something more direct." Clarice seemed more surprised than mad.

"Yeah, like giving you one of those games where you have to dance really fast," Julia said. "That's what got Mr. Fairford last summer. If I wanted to break your ankle, that's how I'd do it."

"Good to know," Clarice told Julia dryly. "Fiona, I'm well aware that an accident is an accident, whether or not it happens in the presence of art."

Elfine smiled. She reached forward and squeezed Clarice's hand.

"Glad to hear it," I told her. I didn't dare tell her just how glad I was or why, though.

"Thank you for your service to the Cold Hope Festival,"

Clarice said, nodding like she really was a queen. "I'll be in touch when I need your help again."

"Bye, Reuben!" Julia said, scratching the cat on his head. Clarice didn't say not to, so I petted his head a little bit, too. He started to purr. For a minute, I felt like maybe things would turn out okay after all.

17

AUNT BECKY WAS probably glad to hear the bakery competition was on. She didn't say thanks or anything. She just nodded and started scribbling some notes.

Great-Uncle Tim looked like he had some mixed feelings about it, though.

"What's up?" I asked him. "Don't you like the festival?"

He shrugged and shook his head.

"Can you draw us a comic so we understand?" I asked.

He hesitated, then nodded. In between helping customers, he started drawing it.

The first box of his comic had balloons and sunshine and "Last Year's Festival" on a big sign. Then there was the bakery competition. Aunt Becky was there, but she looked unhappy. Probably because she was standing in front of a plate of plain old chocolate chip cookies.

The next box was the parade. Great-Uncle Tim and Aunt Becky were marching by themselves with a banner that said

STARKE BROS. BAKERY—THE LEGACY LIVES ON. They didn't look happy about that, either.

After that was the concert. Great-Aunt Alta was in her element, black dress flapping, mouth wide open. She was hitting some huge drums. Aunt Becky and Great-Uncle Tim had their eyes on their shoes. He was playing a recorder, and she was holding a triangle. I guess they were probably playing that song Kevin told me about.

The final panel was a calendar, with this year's festival day outlined in a big storm cloud.

I set the comic down on the counter, confused. "What do chocolate chip cookies have to do with anything? Aren't we past all that?"

"You aren't really going to enter chocolate chip cookies again, are you?" Julia asked Aunt Becky. "That isn't your thing anymore, is it? How would you win a duel with those?"

Aunt Becky stopped the mixer. She came over, stared down at the comic, and sighed. "They were Fiona's grandfather's favorite."

"But . . . he's dead. It's not like he's going to eat any." I frowned. "Wait, let me guess—you play his favorite song. And the parade sign has something to do with him?"

Aunt Becky nodded. Great-Uncle Tim was busy drawing something.

"So every year you do what *he* used to like to do, instead of what *you* want to do? And you've been doing this ever since he died? Since before I was born?"

"You guys know that's weird, right?" Julia asked.

"Yeah," I said. "I mean, he was my granddad, and Mom and I don't do anything like that. Is it what he wanted, do you think?"

Great-Uncle Tim passed me his paper. In one box was a laughing kid sprawled on a couch, eating cookies with his little brother and sister. The little brother was drawing. The sister was banging on the bottom of a pot with a spoon. I could tell that was Great-Aunt Alta, because she looked like a tiny, happy bat.

In the next box was the sad festival stuff they'd been doing.

I was pretty sure the laughing guy wouldn't have wanted this.

Aunt Becky sighed. "My mother . . . Well, she really isn't very good at change."

Good thing I'd had a lot of practice speaking my truths lately. "Yeah, I know. She might not like it if you do something else. But she's not the boss of you," I told them quietly but firmly. "What she wants isn't more important than what you want. She's had things her way for years and years. Why shouldn't it be your turn now? She's not going to get any better at change without practicing. So unless you want to keep doing the same thing for the rest of your lives just because she wants to, I think you'd better try something new."

Aunt Becky stared at the comic for a long time. Then she held out her hand, palm up.

Great-Uncle Tim put his pencil into her hand.

She drew a big X through the chocolate-chip-cookie box. Then she flipped the paper over and drew her own box. It didn't look like she'd worked on her art as much as he had—the arms were in a funny place, and I had no idea what her stick figure was carrying. Something big, with a lot of comic-book sparkles coming off it. But it made her stick figure's smile go right off her head.

We all looked at it for a minute. Then Great-Uncle Tim gave her a smile almost as wide as in her comic.

Aunt Becky flipped the comic back over and made an X through the parade box, too. She left Great-Aunt Alta and the concert alone, though.

She nodded once, sharply. "We'll do the song for her, but not the rest. Are you in?" she asked Great-Uncle Tim.

Slowly, he nodded.

"What are you going to bake instead?" Julia asked.

Aunt Becky smiled. She didn't answer. She just went back to the mixer and turned it up to extra loud.

Honestly, I didn't even know why I bothered trying to help Aunt Becky. It worked better to just ask what she wants to bake and get out of her way.

THAT NIGHT, WHEN WE WERE ALL SITTING AT THE TABLE, SILENTLY eating Great-Aunt Alta's meat loaf (which was actually pretty good—she put barbecue sauce on the top instead of ketchup), I decided we'd better sort a few things out. Otherwise, Aunt Becky and Great-Uncle Tim might lose their nerve and go back to their weird frozen-in-time lives.

I waited until I'd finished my meat loaf, in case Great-Aunt Alta started yelling and I had to go to my room. When I was ready, I took a deep breath. "I think you should know there will be some changes to the festival this year."

Aunt Becky looked shocked. Then she frowned at me. "Right. . . . Since Clarice broke her ankle, other people will be helping out with this year's festival."

Great-Aunt Alta put her fork down and glared at all of us. I could see what writers meant when they said that someone "had a face like thunder." It meant she had eyebrows like dark clouds, and if she could shoot lightning out of her nose, she would.

I took another breath. "Yeah, that too, I guess. But what I really thought you should know—"

Great-Aunt Alta interrupted me. "I will manage the concert."

Aunt Becky looked as shocked as I felt. Great-Uncle Tim looked like he would really, really rather be out in his shed. Maybe I should have warned him or waited until he finished his meat loaf, too.

"Uh, that's okay," I said. "Elfine's going to run it."

"Elfine Dumond?" Great-Aunt Alta sniffed. "It's far too big a responsibility for her to manage on her own. I will run it. She may assist me."

Something told me Elfine wasn't going to be all that into Great-Aunt Alta's plan. But I didn't see how I could fix that. And I hadn't even gotten to the part I was trying to fix yet.

Aunt Becky and Great-Uncle Tim were no help at all. They kept their eyes on their plates. No wonder they'd been doing the same boring things for years.

Great-Aunt Alta looked at me. She looked . . . well, not happy, exactly. But like maybe she had a little less lightning up her nose.

"Aunt Becky needs to bake something different for this year's contest so she can win a duel with her friend Annie. And they're not going to do the parade thing," I said, holding Great-Aunt Alta's almost-glare so she'd know I meant it. "They'll still help you with your song, though. They know that's important to you, and it would be hard to play it all by yourself, with just your drums."

Aunt Becky glanced up at me, and then at her mom. She didn't say anything at all.

Great-Aunt Alta sucked in her breath, then puffed out her cheeks like one of those drawings of the North Wind. Her eyebrows went stormy again.

But I was faster. "Sometimes I don't like it when things change, either," I said quietly but firmly, just like I'd practiced with Ms. Davis and now with Mr. Rivera. "I'm sorry you and my granddad didn't get to work things out before he died. But I really don't think he would want Aunt Becky and Great-Uncle Tim to give up what they want to do on his account. Maybe those things were his favorites when he was alive. You should still remember him and what he liked. But now you should do your own favorite things." I held her glare until she let all her breath back out again. "Is his favorite song really your favorite, too?" I asked. "Or do you want to play a different song this year?"

It was kind of like when I set Aunt Becky off about baking something. *"Also sprach Zarathustra* is not just some song! It's a masterpiece!" Great-Aunt Alta said in the kind of voice that would get a talking-to for being too loud if we were at school. But I saw that even though she wasn't smiling, she wasn't mad anymore, either, and the lava stayed out of my blood.

"I don't know that one. How does it go?" I asked. "Can you sing it?"

Great-Aunt Alta took another deep, deep breath. "Finish your meal," she said, definitely more like an evil queen than a witch. "We must practice."

After dinner, she disappeared up into the attic. After some clunking and thumping around up there, she came back down with a big drum on thin legs. She made three more trips for three more drums and some mallets. (I offered to help, but she said she would handle it.) Aunt Becky and Great-Uncle Tim got their instruments, too. And then . . . they made a racket. I don't know if the song was supposed to sound like that or if they just needed a *lot* more practice. Or maybe some songs are just not meant to be played on a recorder, a triangle, and some huge drums, especially when the recorder doesn't always do the right notes and sometimes the triangle is thinking about baking stuff instead of playing and forgets to do her part.

But Great-Aunt Alta didn't seem to care. She still didn't smile. But she nodded to Aunt Becky when she remembered to play her part, and when she reminded Great-Uncle Tim that it was "duh . . . duh . . . *duh* . . ." instead of "duh . . . duh . . . *whoopswrongnote*," she sounded almost helpful.

I still didn't think she should only ever play one song, though, and only once a year. We were going to have to work on that.

THE NEXT MORNING, I WAS WAITING OUTSIDE THE LIBRARY WHEN Kevin opened it. I checked my email first thing. Ms. Davis hadn't responded yet. Mom had.

Dearest Fiona,

I know I promised you I'd try this program, but it's not helping. I miss you so much. You're such a brave girl, but I bet you're ready to go home now, too. I know you never wanted your summer to be like this.

Why don't you give that Ms. Davis a call for me? Tell her this idea of hers didn't work and you need her to pick me up from here and drive me home so I can get the car. Then I'll come get you, and everything will go back to the way it used to be. We've got each other—we don't need anybody else. You're the best helper a mom could ever have.

I can't wait to see you!

Love,
Mom

18

I READ MOM'S email one more time. I wanted to believe her so much. . . . But the cannonball in my stomach was back, and this time it brought its friends. They were stacked up all the way to the top of my throat. (Yes, I know that's ridiculous. I told my stomach that, too. It didn't help.) And my heart said, *No, don't make that call.* Why not, though? Wouldn't Mom's program have told her if this was really a bad idea? Was I just mad at her for changing the plan again, or was I not feeling very helpful?

My blood wasn't full of lava this time. It was full of bees instead, or wasps, I guess—buzzing and moving around and maybe dangerous or maybe not. I didn't have a checklist for wasps.

I thought about my lava one instead. Sometimes you just have to work with what you have.

1. Do I feel like someone might get hurt?

Not me, safe here in the library. But what about my mom?

What if I didn't call Ms. Davis, and she decided to leave on her own?

I left that one blank for now.

2. Will things get better faster if I call an adult I trust?

I really wished I could walk some laps with Ms. Davis. If I was just being unhelpful, she'd tell me, and then she'd go get my mom. I could almost feel her hands on my shoulders. *Breathe,* she said in my mind. *You've got this. But you have to breathe, Fiona.*

I took a long, deep breath, missing Ms. Davis so hard

it hurt. Why wasn't she there for me when I needed her? I wanted to talk it over with her until all the wasps flew out, far away. My heart filled up with a deep wave of sadness, rattling the cannonballs around. I was all mixed up—so mad that my mom wasn't following the plan we'd made, that she was making me figure this out when I was all alone, without my fairy godmother to help me.

The imaginary Ms. Davis in my mind raised an eyebrow at that.

And as I took another breath, I remembered: I *wasn't* alone with this. I didn't just have a fairy godmother—I had another fairy godperson, too. Did I trust him to help me with this?

Yeah. I did.

3. Is my brain giving me extra energy that helps me? Or extra energy that gets in my way?

Honestly, I didn't care that much, I decided. Whatever it was, a few laps would help.

I went up to the desk. "Can I use the phone?" I asked Kevin. "I need to call Mr. Rivera."

KEVIN HELPED ME FIND SOME FUNNY BOOKS WHILE WE WAITED FOR Mr. Rivera to get there. He didn't try to talk me out of it when I said I wanted to reread some of my favorites. Sometimes I just don't want any more surprises.

Mr. Rivera came in while Kevin was checking out my books. I gave him the printout of Mom's email. He read it while I wrote down my due dates and stuffed all my books in my backpack. I told Kevin thanks, and that maybe I'd see him later.

When Mr. Rivera finished reading, he gave Mom's email back to me. "I called Becky and told her we were going to the track," he said. "It's a great idea. I could use some exercise."

"So can Ms. Davis," I told him as we left the library. "That's why we do it. Well, part of it." I explained about the bees, or maybe wasps.

"I wonder what the difference is between bees and wasps?" he said.

I settled into his car and buckled up. "Bees are hairy with flat legs. They collect pollen," I told him. "Wasps are skinny in the middle and are predators, and they make paper houses. Kevin didn't know, either, so he helped me look it up. There was a lot more about them, but we think those are the basics."

He nodded thoughtfully. "And bees make honey, right?"

"Some do. Others pollinate stuff. I don't think wasps do that." I stared out the window as he pulled into a small school parking lot. No one else was there.

"Sounds like it could be hard to tell which is buzzing around inside you," he said. "Something helpful or something not."

I nodded. We got out of the car and headed over to the track.

Walking felt good, even though those insects were still buzzing around. It felt like getting back to something right, something normal. A good kind of normal. "I should be happy about my mom's email," I said after we'd walked around a few times. There's no hurry when you're walking laps. After all, more is better for you. "But I'm not. I don't know why I'm not happy about it."

Mr. Rivera sighed. "Some situations aren't so clear. I know you really miss your mom, and I want you to be back with her as soon as possible. But I also really want her to get the help she needs. I worry that things might be hard for you if she doesn't."

"Me too," I said quietly. All those insects were settling down some now, lulled by the sound of our sneakers on the packed earth of the track, slow and steady, like a calm heartbeat.

I could feel the sun coming in through my skin, warming up the cold parts inside me. Good thing I'd put on my sunblock. "I want her to be right," I said after a while. "She's my mom, and I should trust her. But sometimes . . . she gets things wrong." I didn't look at his face. I didn't want to know what he thought about that.

"We all get things wrong sometimes," he said. "Even parents. Sometimes we need a reminder from someone else to think about whether we're making a good choice or not. You think Julia never tells me when I make a mistake?"

I looked up at him. He was smiling, though he looked kind of sad, too. He knew that wasn't the same kind of thing. I looked back down at the track stretching out in front of us. "I had plans," I told him. "First, I had plans for my summer— and she changed those. Then I made new plans—and now she wants to change those, too."

"Did you tell her that upset you?" he asked.

I shook my head. "It wouldn't matter."

"How do you know, unless you try?" he asked. "I know it's not easy to tell her what you really think, Fiona. But I suspect she'd be making a mistake to leave early, too. And it doesn't seem fair to you to change the plan now, especially if it means leaving before she finishes the work that's sup- posed to make life better for both of you. If I were her, I'd want to know what you think. Even if it was hard to hear."

We walked a lap in silence. Then he said, "So, shall we make a plan for what you want to tell her?"

I sighed. "Okay. And then . . . Do you think Julia might want to hang out later?"

Dear Mom,

I miss you, too. But I don't think that's a good plan right now.

I promised my friend Julia I'd go to the Cold Hope Festival with her, and if I leave, she'll have to go by herself. And Ms. Davis is off today. I can't just call her and ask her to change all her plans because you're ready to go right now. That's not fair to her.

I want to help you. But I've been helping people here, too. I can't just not show up when they need me. What happens if Aunt Becky loses her baking duel? Who's going to clap for Great-Aunt Alta's terrible song? Maybe I haven't told you about those things yet. Maybe because you forgot to ask how my summer's going.

I love you, Mom. But I'm not going to ask Ms. Davis to pick you up early. Maybe I wasn't so sure about this plan when summer started. But you asked me to help you with it. You said it's what we both needed, even if it was hard for us. I'm doing my part. And I think the best way I can help is to ask you to stay there and give your program some more time.

Love,
Fiona

Dear Ms. Davis,

It's a good thing I know how to speak my truths, because I had to do it again with my mom today. I deserve an A++ for that lesson. Mr. Rivera agrees. I'm really tired of talking about it, so he said he'd fill you in.

I'm going to tell you about my latest fairy-godperson stuff instead. You would not believe the ridiculous things my relatives have been doing. Every year, instead of doing what they want to do at the festival, they do what Great-Aunt Alta thinks my dead grandfather would have wanted them to do! Bake his favorite cookies. . . . Carry a sign in the parade about how they remember him. . . . Play his favorite song in the talent show.

But not this year. This year, Aunt Becky is going to bake something else. I mean, okay, she's focused on winning her ultimate duel with her frenemy, not on baking her coolest recipe. But I guess it's still progress?

I don't know what Great-Uncle Tim is up to. He snuck out again, even though I told him he probably needs to get permission before he draws on any more buildings. Especially now that the police put up wanted posters for his secret artist alter ego. Do you think I should follow him? Tailing someone seems like something a spy would do, not a fairy godperson. Julia says you never know, though—it could still be a useful skill. I guess I'll read up on it when I can. Also, he takes the car, so how could I keep up? I don't know how to hang off the side of a car or anything. So I'm thinking not.

I had a brilliant breakthrough with Great-Aunt Alta, though! I distracted her with music, the same way Aunt Becky gets really into her baking stuff. And it worked! Kind of. Now she doesn't yell when we change things, she just talks and talks and talks about how great this song she likes is. It's about how somebody called Zarathustra said something, and my granddad liked it because it was in a movie he thought was cool. Great-Aunt Alta says it's more than a hundred years old, and people still listen to it! (I don't know why they put such an old song in a movie. Maybe they got it for cheap.) Really, though, she thinks it has a great drum part, and she likes to play the drums.

Julia just got here. She says to tell you I'm going to have fun at the festival for Lesson 3, not just help save it. Julia is a very thorough helper. I'm already learning that it can be kind of tiring when your helper is that relentless. (She says she's sure I'll survive.)

Your apprentice-fairy-godperson-in-training,
Fiona

P.S. I am still fine. I still miss my mom. I told her I love her (again). Along with everything else. Well, some of it.

P.P.S. I guess it's good I'm here, though, because these people would not be managing well at all without me.

19

THE NEXT MORNING, I met Julia at the park near the festival entrance. Aunt Becky was at the bakery, finishing up her ultimate weapon. Great-Uncle Tim was off somewhere, maybe helping her or maybe doing some mysterious and possibly illegal art. Who knew.

"What do you want to do first?" Julia asked.

"Um . . ." I hadn't thought much about it. Not with everyone else's stuff to worry about.

Julia grinned. "No wonder you have to have an assignment to practice having fun! I'll help, though. Let's walk around and see what's here. Then you can figure out what you want to do. We've got plenty of time."

So we watched kids jump around in the bouncy house and farmers get their vegetables and flowers ready to sell, and we waved to Mr. Rivera and his team, busy setting up tables on the grass for the baking-contest entries. "We should probably go check on Aunt Becky," I said.

Julia folded her arms. "Only after we do something that you want to do. For fun, not for helping someone."

"Fine. What do you want to do?"

"You're the one with the assignment! *You* have to pick." She rolled her eyes, but she was still smiling. "Didn't you look at any of the signs we just walked past? There's face painting, or we could go see the alpacas, or get our pictures taken in those big paintings with holes cut out for your face. . . ."

"Alpacas!" I checked the time quickly—we were still okay. "And pictures, too!"

"Extra-credit bonus fun points!" Julia gave me a high five, and we were off.

I didn't exactly forget about Aunt Becky's duel or stop checking my watch. But I managed to have a pretty good time with Julia anyway. I'd never seen real, live alpacas before. They were so cute! They kept peering out at us from under their long, curly bangs to see if maybe we had treats.

"There should be more stories about alpacas," Julia said. "They'd fit right into a fairy tale, don't you think?"

I agreed. So we made some improvements to all the stories we could think of.

" 'The Princess and the Frog . . . and the Alpaca'!" Julia said, grinning.

" 'Beauty and the Alpaca'!" I countered. "Or maybe the Beast has a herd of alpacas living in his castle."

" 'The Three Billy Alpacas Gruff'!" Julia said. "Stomping

across the bridge, looking for treats! There's got to be stories about them. Maybe we just haven't read them yet."

I'd never stuck my face through a hole in a huge painting of a chicken before, either. The lady in charge told us to cluck as loud as we could, and then she took our picture with Julia's phone.

I looked down at my tiny face sticking out through the huge chicken. The girl in the picture looked like any kid having a fun day at a fair. It made me feel kind of uneasy. Like something bad could happen if I didn't get back to work. "I really need to go check on Aunt Becky now," I told Julia, handing back her phone.

"Okay," Julia said. "But only if you come watch the parade with me after."

I could do that. Things would be fine once the duel was over. "Deal," I told her, smiling.

Mr. Rivera and his team had finished covering the baking-competition tables with tablecloths and had put caution tape all around them.

Twenty or so contestants were setting up their cookies and cakes and stuff. I didn't see Aunt Becky or her frenemy yet. But Portia was there, along with a few people I'd helped at the bakery.

"Hey, girls." Mr. Rivera came over and put his arm around Julia's shoulders. "How's the festival?"

"Pretty good," I said.

"Hey, Dad, next year can I enter something?" Julia asked.

"Sure, if I'm not the judge," Mr. Rivera said. "What are you going to make?"

"A poisoned-apple cake!" Julia said.

"No poisoning the judges," Mr. Rivera said immediately. "And no grossing out the judges with something that isn't actually poisonous but tastes really bad. After all, I might have to judge one again someday." He grinned at her.

Julia rolled her eyes. "I know, Dad. It would only look like the poisoned apple—you know, the one in 'Snow White.' A wicked-witch cake—red apple with white inside. I'm thinking coconut." She grinned back.

Mr. Rivera clutched his throat and stuck his tongue out like he was cartoon-dying.

"He hates coconut," Julia told me. "But not as much as I hate raisins. What would you make?"

I thought about it. Magic-wand cakes and glass-slipper cakes sounded hard. Besides, I wanted to be a fairy god-

person in *this* world, not a long time ago. "Maybe a car shaped like a pumpkin," I said. "It could taste like pumpkin, too." I didn't know how to make anything like that. But I bet Julia didn't know how to make an apple cake, either. Not yet. That didn't stop her.

"Nice!" Julia said.

It made me a little sad, though, because I wasn't going to be here next year. And I hadn't even thought about making anything this year. I'd been too busy helping everyone else.

Then I noticed that the other contestants had gotten really, really quiet. Aunt Becky and Annie had arrived.

It was like watching one of those old Western movies. Only, nobody had a hat. (Or a gun, thank goodness.) Aunt Becky walked slowly up to the tables, carrying her entry on a platter in front of her. It looked heavy—there was a *lot* of frosting—but her arms didn't shake. Her eyes didn't leave Annie's.

Annie came up from the other side, carrying her entry, too, staring right back at Aunt Becky.

It was so quiet I wanted to giggle. That happens some-times when I get nervous. I watched them stalk up to the tables and put down their entries across from each other. They still didn't look away.

"You're not from around here, pardner," I whispered to Julia, in my best Western-movie voice.

"This town's not big enough for the both of us," she whispered back. We cracked up.

Maybe that did something to the air, or maybe everyone just lost interest, but people started talking again. I craned my neck to see what Annie had brought.

It was a catapult. It looked like it was made out of cake and pretzel sticks or something, with round frosted boulders that were probably cake, too, for the catapult to launch. It was sitting in a field of green frosting grass, with cookie trees standing all around it.

"How long do you think she spent making that?" I whis-pered.

Julia shrugged. "What's your aunt's entry supposed to be?"

"A castle, I think?" I said. "Or a fortress? That's why the frosting is gray. See—it's got those square things at the top of the castle towers, for archers or whatever."

Julia tipped her head and frowned. "I think I can kind of see it."

Mostly, Aunt Becky's entry just looked like a square

cake with gray frosting and medium and little squares on top. "She got her spice-cake recipe to taste exactly like she wanted, though."

The last few people were bringing their entries to the tables. "Come on—I want to go see what Portia made," Julia said.

Portia had rolled out cookie dough and cut out circles. Every circle was frosted in a different color combination and pattern. Darkest purple with lime-green stripes, pale blue with orange starbursts, sunny yellow with magenta zigzags—I couldn't help but smile.

"That's the exact color I need for my poisoned-apple cake," Julia said, pointing at a deep red cookie with tiny blue dots. "And I want mine to be shiny like that, too."

"I can show you how to mix it anytime and how to paint it on," Portia said.

"What kind of cookies did you make?" I asked.

"My grandmother's brown-sugar cookies," Portia told me. "They aren't fancy, but they're the best." She smiled. "You know, I couldn't stop thinking about that question you asked me, Julia—about what kind of cookie I'd be. You could say these are my answer."

"They're beautiful!" Julia said. "Are you nervous?"

"Nah, I did my part. Now it's time to see what happens." Portia grinned.

Mr. Rivera was walking from entry to entry. For each one,

he took a small bite from the sample on the little plate in front of it. Then he examined the entry and made some notes on his clipboard.

"Clarice gave him a form so he can judge them," Julia said. "Every entry gets two scores, one for how it looks and one for how it tastes."

I wondered if Aunt Becky was nervous. I was nervous for her, with entries like the catapult and Portia's cookies. But she just kept staring at Annie. She'd cut a piece right out of the castle for the judge's sample, so the brown spice cake showed through the cut part. I decided I'd better get her some cake-decorating books from the library the next time I went.

Annie had planned ahead, I could see. She'd made a separate boulder and part of the catapult for her sample so she didn't have to cut up her design. But when Mr. Rivera took a bite, it looked like the cake was just plain yellow. Like, from a mix.

Finally, Mr. Rivera stopped and examined his notes. Slowly, he circled the tables again, writing out a little card for each entry.

The people around us were muttering and whispering, craning their necks to see what happened.

When he finished, he waved a lady from his team over. She was carrying a bag of ribbons.

Mr. Rivera cleared his throat.

The crowd fell silent.

"I would like to thank everyone who entered this year's baking competition," Mr. Rivera said. He wasn't yelling, but his voice carried, clear and strong. "We are lucky to have so many talented bakers in town—even if it does make my job harder!" A few people laughed at that, and Mr. Rivera grinned.

And I realized something: he wasn't nervous. He didn't look like he was worried about what Aunt Becky and Annie were up to. He looked like he was having fun, doing something he wanted to do.

I don't know why that was such a surprise to me. Maybe because when I imagined myself helping other people, I never thought about how I would feel, only about how they would. I knew Clarice was glad he was helping her out, and so were Aunt Becky and Annie and probably everyone else here who'd made something. But I hadn't thought that maybe Mr. Rivera would be glad, too. (Even if he didn't want to do it every single time.)

"This year we're introducing something new," Mr. Rivera went on. "I'll be awarding two special ribbons in addition to the grand prize. First up: the award for excellence in appearance. The winner is . . . Annie Simmons for her entry, 'Cake Catapult.'"

Everyone clapped and cheered, even me and Julia. Even Aunt Becky. I mean, she wasn't jumping up and down and woo-hooing. But at least she was being a good sport.

"Next, the award for excellence in taste," Mr. Rivera continued. "The winner is . . . Becky Starke for her entry, 'Spice Castle with Caramel Cream-Cheese Frosting.'"

Everyone clapped and cheered for Aunt Becky, too—even Annie. I saw Aunt Becky glance up, startled. She stood there for a moment, kind of frozen. And then she smiled. It made me feel warm inside, like I'd just eaten one of her blueberry bran muffins.

And then everyone got very quiet. Mr. Rivera still didn't look nervous, but I was. Who was going to win this duel? My stomach went from warm and happy to full of cannonballs. If Aunt Becky won it, she'd never say sorry for real. And if Annie won it, she probably wouldn't, either. So how was this going to make anything better?

Mr. Rivera looked down at his notes again. "It is my honor to announce this year's grand-prize winner," he said, and smiled. "Portia Allen for her entry, 'Brown-Sugar Cookies with Patterns in Cardamom.' Congratulations, Portia!"

My mouth fell right open. I stared at him.

Mr. Rivera handed Portia her blue ribbon. She said something I couldn't hear, and they both laughed.

"Go, Portia!" Julia hollered, jumping up and down and cheering.

"Who wants to try a blue-ribbon cookie?" Portia asked. She smiled and held out her plate.

And before I knew it, I was clapping and jumping up and down for Portia, too, the cheers pouring out of me. Because Portia wasn't out to win a duel. Portia wasn't about being better than someone else or being right. She didn't have a fairy godperson, and she didn't need one. She just worked hard, helped herself, and made the best cookies she could.

Aunt Becky stared at me. Then she looked away.

And . . . I didn't go help her.

Because I realized something: Aunt Becky already had everything she needed. Her friend was right there. She knew how to apologize.

She just didn't want to.

It made me furious. Here I'd been trying and trying to help her, and she hadn't done her part at all. She'd just kept fighting instead of fixing things. And I'd let her. I'd pretended things were getting better when really they weren't. And I was sick of it. Helping people was hard—way harder than I'd thought. And if they were just going to keep doing their same old things that they knew didn't work . . .

I was done.

So when Julia pulled me over toward Portia, I went without looking back. "I'm glad you won," I told her. And I meant it.

Portia grinned. "Thanks. Try one."

Julia picked the dark red one with the little blue dots. I picked the blue one with orange stars.

And you know what? It was as delicious as it was beautiful.

"Great job, Dad!" Julia said, grinning up at Mr. Rivera. She gave him a hug. Suddenly, I missed my mom so much. It felt hard and sharp and sweet as a flaming-sword pie through my heart.

But I didn't have time for that right then, so I set those feelings aside for later. "Yeah, great job, Mr. Rivera," I told him. I wanted him to know I wasn't mad that he hadn't given the prize to Aunt Becky.

Then, out of the corner of my eye, I saw Aunt Becky take a step toward Annie. I tried not to look. But I couldn't help myself.

Aunt Becky said something too quiet for me to hear.

Annie turned and glared at her. "What did you say?"

This time, Aunt Becky spoke up. "I said, I guess you'll finally have to admit that I was right. Taste does matter." She folded her arms and glared back at her frenemy.

I could feel the tension building up in my body, making my nerves feel like wires.

"You doing okay, Fiona?" Mr. Rivera asked.

I took a deep, slow breath, the kind that reminds my body that I'm a person and it had better not try to turn me into some lava factory.

"Yeah, is this the part where we do something?" Julia asked.

Aunt Becky and Annie were really arguing now.

I watched them, letting my feelings swirl around inside me. I couldn't wave a magic wand and make those feelings vanish. But I didn't have to do what they wanted me to, either.

"I'm fine," I told Mr. Rivera, turning away from the argument, back to my friend. "If they're going to fight, there's nothing I can do to stop it. They know how to apologize— when they're ready." I shrugged. My stomach felt bad, but it wouldn't kill me. There was still some lava trying to get into my blood; I couldn't make that vanish, either. But lava has no place in a baking competition.

"Come on," I told Julia. "Let's go have fun."

She grinned at me, and I felt the lava slowly pulling back. "Okay! Dad, Fiona and I are going to watch the parade together."

"You want me to come with?" he asked. "I'll just be a moment."

"Nah, we're good," Julia said.

He nodded. "Text me if you need me."

She turned back to me. "Let's go claim our spot!"

And then her eyes went wide. I turned to see—just as Annie's hand came down on her catapult. It was loaded.

We stared as a boulder the size of a cupcake flew over the

grass. It hit Aunt Becky square in the face, smashing into a smear of frosting and crumbs.

Aunt Becky didn't have a catapult. She just grabbed a handful of cake and threw it straight at Annie. Her aim was pretty good, too.

All around us, people yelled and scrambled out of the way, yanking their baked goods to safety. Mr. Rivera tried to say something over all the noise, but I couldn't hear what. Cake was flying. I couldn't move, couldn't think—and then Julia grabbed my hand. She was smiling. "This is way better than boring old chocolate chip cookies!" she shouted.

And as I clutched Julia's hand, Aunt Becky wiped the frosting and crumbs off her face with her apron and started

to laugh. Annie stared at her, and then she started laughing, too. They crossed the frosting-splattered grass to each other, but not like gunslingers this time. Instead, they hugged, careless of the mess, like friends who hadn't seen each other in ages.

20

AS I FOLLOWED Julia across the park, I felt my cannonballs of worry fall apart into cake crumbs. I didn't really understand it, but Aunt Becky was going to be okay. She was maybe even going to be friends with Annie again. Slowly, my blood cooled back down. My stomach felt strange and kind of empty, like I wasn't sure what to do without all that weight. It had been a while since I just got to hang out with a friend without trying to fix anything. Not since . . . I gave up and followed Julia's lead.

Julia's favorite spot to watch the parade was near the platform where Renee was going to do her announcing. "If you're too close to where the parade starts, the people throwing candy haven't really got the hang of it yet—they're worried about running out," she explained as we walked toward the platform. "By the time they get here, they know what to do."

The street was blocked off with cones and barriers, so no cars accidentally joined the parade. Adults were sitting all along the curb, talking to each other, and little kids were running around in the street, exactly like they weren't supposed to do on a normal day. But Julia's spot was waiting for us. Maybe because the bench was covered with signs that said "This Spot Reserved for the Most Magical, Most Dangerous People in Fairy Tales." Or maybe because there was a guy guarding it for us. He was really, really tall, with long black hair and wide muscly shoulders and extra-fierce eyebrows. No one would mess with him, even if he was wearing a T-shirt that said "Vegans for Peace," with a lot of fluffy bunnies and glitter peace signs on it. As soon as he saw Julia, his face lit up into a grin. Julia had a lot of friends here. I was glad she'd decided to be my friend, too.

"Thanks for saving our spot, Jason," Julia said. "This is my friend Fiona. Want to sit with us? There's room."

He shook his head. "Thanks, but I have to get ready to march with my cooking club." He hesitated, then leaned over to whisper to us, practically bending double to get his head down by Julia's ear. "Portia said to tell you that Entry Twenty-One will be worth the wait." He straightened up and grinned again.

"Got it. Good luck!" Julia said, grinning back.

We waved as he hurried down the street.

Then Julia carefully peeled the sign off the back of the bench. There was one of those little metal plaques underneath. This one read "In memory of Flor and Daniel Martin, who loved to watch the parade." Julia patted the plaque and settled onto the bench next to it, not blocking it at all.

I sat down next to her. I could tell this was important, even if I didn't know why. "Did you know them?"

She nodded, not looking at me. "They were my parents. They died in a car accident, a long time ago."

"But . . ." I made myself think before I said anything dumb. I knew Julia was Mr. Rivera's daughter. I just hadn't known she had different parents before that. "I'm sorry. Do you miss them?"

She nodded again. "I don't remember them that well now," she said, really quietly. "But I still miss what I remember. I like to watch the parade here. But you don't have to, if you don't want to."

I hadn't known Julia very long. I didn't know if she wanted company when she felt sad. But sometimes you just have to do your best.

I reached out, grabbed her hand, and squeezed it. "I still want to watch the parade with you, if you're good with that."

"Thanks." She smiled, still a little sad. "I'd like that."

It seemed like a good time to speak my truth, too. "I miss my mom today. She's not dead. She had to go stay with people who know how to help her, maybe. I hope. And I had to come here while they try." I looked down at our hands. "I tried and tried. But I couldn't break her curse."

"I'm sorry." Julia squeezed my hand. "I wish magic could just fix everything. I hate that it can't." She was quiet for a moment. Then she said, "But I'm glad we get to hang out today."

"Me too," I said. It was weird to think that I might never have come here and met her.

We sat there in silence for a while. And then Julia grabbed my arm and pointed up at the platform.

Renee stepped forward and tapped one of the microphones. She wasn't wearing her postal-carrier outfit. Instead, she was wearing a long dress with so many colors packed in, it was way beyond the rainbow. She had a hat, too, with a matching scarf tied around it.

"I bet she made that herself," Julia whispered. "She knows how to sew."

I nodded. You couldn't just go buy a dress like that at a store. With the wind billowing it out around her, she looked like someone out of a cartoon—a superhero or a princess or some combination of both—although I still thought her true form was a dragon. Just like the Bakesy painting on the post-office wall behind her.

"Welcome to the forty-first annual Cold Hope Festival

Parade!" Renee's voice boomed out through the speakers set up around the stage. "We will be starting at two p.m. sharp—in less than five minutes!" Her voice was warm, confident, and totally no-nonsense. "Participants, take your places. As in past years, if I see anyone joining their group after the parade begins, I will tell an embarrassing story about that person into the microphone so everyone can hear. Consider yourselves warned!"

Julia and I watched as panicked people ran for the start of the parade. "Does she really do that?" I asked.

Julia nodded. "They're really good stories, too! I hope someone's late again this year."

It was kind of like other parades I'd seen, and also kind of not. There were fewer big fancy floats than in city parades, but there was more candy-throwing and more groups of people jogging by, all wearing identical T-shirts with words too small to read from where we were sitting. We waved at them anyway, and Julia helped me figure out the ones she knew.

"I didn't know we had a pirate fan club! No, wait—they've got burgers on the backs of their shirts. Whoa, they're on roller skates! I think it's the new roller-derby team!" We cheered and clapped as the pirates rolled by, backward, amid cries of "Arr!" and "Aye, matey!" The person with a star on her pirate helmet unfurled a banner that read, "Thanks to M&G Burgers for sponsoring our team!"

The high school drama club did a whole song and dance on the back of one of those big flatbed trucks. We were pretty impressed that no one fell off and got a concussion. Plus, you could hear their tap shoes from all the way down the street. "That'll be me someday," Julia said, her eyes shining as she watched them leap and twirl. "Evillene or Miss One or Elphaba or Glinda . . ."

A group of kids with shin guards and either Godzilla masks or skyscraper hats dribbled soccer balls around a guy who was towing a wagon with the longest sandwich I'd ever seen.

"Perry's Deli always sponsors a team," Julia told me. "Their six-foot-long sandwiches are great."

"Why Godzilla?" I asked.

She shrugged. "Teams get to pick their own names. They have to wear their regular uniforms for games, though."

I tore my gaze from the sandwich, bouncing along in its wagon, occasionally throwing out a splash of mustard or slice of pickle, and looked to see what was next. Suddenly, everyone went quiet, even Renee.

A big truck was coming down the street. On the back was a float. It was an enormous dragon, done in papier-mâché or something, painted in splashes of every color you could think of—as many colors as there were in Renee's dress.

As the float rolled along, I could see that the dragon was

curled around a heap of huge sparkling flowers. Just like in the Bakesy painting on the post office, right behind Renee. The dragon's mouth opened and shut, and orange-painted flames rolled in and out, like banners.

And there was a statue of a person standing in front of the dragon, so close that the flame banners almost hit them. They were holding up a rose, and it was painted in every color at once, too.

I looked at Julia. She looked at me. "That's the coolest thing I've ever seen!" she breathed. "Did you help him with this? How did he make it move?"

I shook my head. It was amazing . . . but it had trouble written all over it, even if no one broke their ankle this time.

People were looking from the dragon to the post-office wall and back again. They'd figured it out.

So had Renee. "Next we have one of the most innova-

tive floats this emcee has ever seen," she said, smiling, and totally ignoring the huge, probably illegal painting on the wall behind her. She adjusted her rainbow reading glasses and looked at her notes. "It's called 'What Can You Give a Dragon?' and it's by Cold Hope's very own master of anonymous art. Let's give it up for . . . Bakesy!"

My stomach was all twisted up inside, but I let out the loudest cheer I could anyway. So did Julia. And so did the crowd around us. Adults were staring, but they were smiling, too. Little kids opened and closed their mouths in time with the dragon as it rolled past.

Then Julia elbowed me and pointed at the stage.

Renee was arguing with a police officer. She flicked her microphone back on, her face stormy. "Apparently, *some people* do not understand the prestige an artist like Bakesy can bring to a town! I mean, really. . . . *Some people* wouldn't know a city-beautification project if it bit them!" Her voice boomed out over the crowd. People started to mutter. Renee rolled her eyes. "Driver, can you please state whether you are or are not the anonymous artist known as Bakesy?"

The truck slowed, then stopped. As the driver's window

rolled down, my heart banged around inside me like a pin-ball machine.

But it wasn't Great-Uncle Tim. Instead, Elfine stuck her head out. "I wish this *was* mine, but it isn't!" she yelled up at Renee. "I was asked to drive Float Twenty-One, since I'm licensed to drive commercial trucks. That's all I know about it."

The police officer made a move like he was going to step off the stage and go ask her a few questions anyway. But Elfine just rolled up her window and started slowly driving forward.

Renee glared at him. "Whoever made this float could be anywhere by now."

But just then the dragon gave an ominous creak. The truck stopped. The dragon's lower jaw fell off with a crack, crushing the statue in front of it . . . and revealing Great-Uncle Tim standing inside the dragon's broken head.

I grabbed Julia's hand and hung on tight. "Uh-oh." No magic wand was going to get us out of this one—even if I had one. Which I didn't.

Julia squeezed back. "I'll text my dad."

Everyone else cheered. I don't know if they thought Great-Uncle Tim's sudden appearance was part of the performance or what. But they were into it.

Great-Uncle Tim dropped the ropes he was holding. It looked like they were controlling some kind of pulley system for the dragon's mouth, and maybe the flames, too. He climbed over the dragon's fallen jaw and bent over, searching through the wreckage for something.

"Bill, I'm telling you, this is an *important moment*," Renee hissed at the police officer. If she'd had a dragon tail, it would have been twitching. "I know you've got your duty, but trust me, he's not going anywhere. If you take one step off this stage, I will tell everyone the story of when you tried to take a nap in the back of the police car and locked yourself in, and Clarice and I had to get you out with a coat hanger." The microphone picked up every word she said.

Bill the police officer stopped, but he didn't take his eyes off Great-Uncle Tim.

Great-Uncle Tim straightened up. I could see what he was holding now: the colorful papier-mâché rose. It only looked a little bit squashed. Carefully, he climbed down off the truck and walked to the stage. He held up the rose in front of Renee, just like the statue had held it up in front of the dragon.

Renee still had the microphone. And since Julia and I were listening instead of talking, we heard her when she whispered "Yes" as she bent down to take the rose.

"You're under arrest!" Bill the police officer barked at Great-Uncle Tim.

21

I GRABBED JULIA'S hand and ran, dragging her behind me. It wasn't a fairy-godperson thing to do at all. But I had to get away. I couldn't watch everything go wrong again. We fled down the street, through the park, up a hill, under some trees. I was tired, and I didn't know what to do. Finally, I stopped running.

Julia was breathing hard. "That dragon was the best!" she said. "I mean, okay, maybe it could be sturdier next time. But it was the coolest, for sure!"

I sagged against a tree trunk. "How can there be a next time? He got caught! He got *arrested*!"

"Only a little bit." Julia shrugged. "I mean, sure, he'll have to fix his mistakes. But my dad will help him find something that's not so illegal to do with his art, I bet. It's not like anybody got crushed to death or anything." She studied my face. "What's wrong?"

"Things just keep falling apart," I said, wiping my sleeve

across my eyes fast so maybe she wouldn't see. "Every time I try to help, they get all messed up."

"Are you sure?" Julia asked. She sat down on a big rock and patted the spot next to her. "Remind me—what was your great-uncle like when you came here?"

I sat down next to her and tried to remember. "He never got arrested before."

"That's because your relatives never did anything interesting," Julia pointed out. "They just moped around, like Cinderella and her ashes or Sleeping Beauty in the middle of those thorns. What kind of fairy godperson would leave them like that without changing things up?"

"Yeah, but those fairy godpeople were experts, not apprentices," I argued. "They knew how to give people their happily-ever-afters."

"And nothing ever got messed up along the way?" Julia said. "I mean, if some fairy left me sitting by the road in the middle of the night with a pumpkin, some rodents, and only one shoe, I wouldn't be that impressed. But that wasn't the fairy godmother's fault. She told that girl to watch the clock. And when Cinderella didn't pay attention, she didn't step in and save her. People have to learn from their mistakes." She thought about it for a minute. "Okay, the glass shoes were totally her fault. I mean, who gives people breakable shoes? That girl is lucky she didn't lose a foot."

It was hard to argue with Julia. She knew the stories as well as I did. "You sound like Portia."

She grinned. "I try." She jumped to her feet. "Look, you can help get people moving, but they get to do their own thing after that. Even if it's not what you wanted. What do you think Cinderella's fairy godmother did while she was moping around waiting for some guy to bring her stupid shoe back?"

I'd never really thought about that before. "Helped someone else, I guess."

"Well, my dad texted that he'll help your great-uncle, and nobody else here needs help." She put her hands on her hips. "What if you had fun with your friend the usually good witch instead? I know, people don't tell stories about that. But that's probably because everything goes right, with no drama at all."

"I shouldn't." I peered out through the trees at the festival.

"If your fairy godmother was here, what would she say you should do?" Julia asked. "Wait—she already told you! Lesson Three!" She pulled out her notebook and flipped it open.

I took it and read what she'd written: "Fiona wants to go to the festival and have fun—and not help anyone."

"There's your signature, in fake blood and everything. You have to do it. So, no more moping around like some princess," Julia said. "Not when you have an assignment to do!"

DON'T EVEN BOTHER TRYING TO ARGUE WITH A WITCH. ESPECIALLY NOT one who's trying to be a force for good, whether you want her to or not.

My stomach did calm down a little while we drew brooms and wands and poisoned apples and pumpkin coaches for the huge chalk-art project that covered most of Park Avenue.

As we waited in line to dunk Julia's school principal in the dunk tank, Mr. Rivera texted again to tell us that Great-Uncle Tim would be okay. He'd probably have to do some community service and stuff, but he wasn't going to jail. My ball still wobbled some when I threw it, but at least the lava had cooled down. And Julia's throw didn't do much better, not even after she whispered some secret magical words. But we got to cheer with everyone else when the next kid in line sent the principal right into the tank.

Slowly, slowly, the rest of the weight and worry trickled out while we Hula-Hooped with, like, a billion other people on the baseball field. The high school marching band went around and around, playing that "Do Wah Diddy" song, over and over and over. We all sang at the top of our lungs. Nobody knew the words.

Then we passed our hoops on to some other people who wanted in. Julia was teaching me how to make dandelion chains when her phone buzzed. "Are you ready to go find seats for the concert?" she asked me. "It's early, but my dad wants us to meet him now."

"Sure," I said, tying the end of my chain to the first dandelion and hanging it around my neck. I got up and brushed off my shorts.

Julia held out her hands, and I hauled her to her feet.

The dandelion chain on her head slipped down over one eye and made us laugh.

She straightened it. "Come on."

AS SOON AS I SAW MR. RIVERA WAITING FOR US, MY STOMACH DROPPED down into my shoes. I know what it looks like when someone has something they don't want to tell you.

I ran to him. "Is it my mom?" I asked, breathing hard. "Is she okay?" Everything was falling apart again while I was off having fun. I was definitely the worst fairy godperson ever.

"Here she is," Mr. Rivera said into his phone. "Hang on a sec." He took the phone away from his ear and met my eyes. "Your mom's fine for now, Fiona. We're just trying to figure out how to help her keep herself that way." His voice was calm and slow, but my breathing didn't care. "Julia, hold this for me for a minute, okay?" He handed her the phone, and put his hands on my shoulders.

I could feel the lava in my blood rising and rising, building up, like a volcano. Just because you can watch it move doesn't mean you can stop it from overflowing. "But I emailed her! I told her what I thought, just like you said!" My voice didn't sound like mine anymore. "What went wrong?"

Some noise was coming out of the phone. Julia held it up to her ear. Then she pushed a button, and I could hear Ms. Davis's voice.

"Fiona, breathe with me," she commanded.

I was so surprised to hear her that I did what she asked, hiccupping through my sobs. In and hold. Out.

Julia grabbed my hand tight, and she breathed, too. So did Mr. Rivera.

"I'm sorry this is scaring you, Fiona," Ms. Davis went on. "Mr. Rivera is right—things are fine for now."

"Promise?" I asked, forcing the word past the lump in my throat.

"I promise," she said. "I will never lie to you. You know that, right?"

"Is that your fairy godperson?" Julia whispered, her eyes wide.

"Yeah," I whispered back.

"Is that Julia I hear in the background?" Ms. Davis asked.

"Yeah!" Julia said. "I put it on speaker like you said. Do you need me to go away so you can talk to Fiona?"

"Nice to meet you, Julia," Ms. Davis said. "Thank you for following directions—I appreciate your help. . . . Fiona, Mr. Rivera and I need to talk to you about your mom. Would you rather have Julia stay here or give us some space for a little while?"

"It's okay either way," Julia whispered. "I won't be mad."

I squeezed her hand. "Can you stay?"

"Sure," she said, and squeezed back.

Mr. Rivera nodded. "Fiona, like we were saying, your mom is safe. She's at her treatment program now. But she called Ms. Davis because she wants to leave early and come get you."

"But I told her not to!" I said, feeling my blood heat up again. "I emailed her and told her!"

"You did great," he said seriously. "You spoke your truth, just like Ms. Davis taught you. None of this is your fault. We need you to keep breathing, okay? We have time to talk this through and make some decisions." He took a deep breath, and so did I.

"Why can't she just do what she's supposed to do?" I asked. "She promised!"

"Because this is hard stuff she's struggling with," Mr. Rivera said. "I believe that she's trying. But addiction gets in the way." He took another long, slow breath. "That's why it's important for her to stay where she can get help with it."

I took a breath. Julia's hand was still tight in mine. "When is she coming?" I asked. "Do I have to leave tonight?"

"Fiona, your mom hasn't left her program yet," Ms. Davis said. "We want you to have the opportunity to tell her what you think first, if you want to. You don't have to. But if you have something to say, Mr. Rivera will call the program for you and you can talk to her."

"But she never listens to me!" I said. "She wants every-thing to go back the way it was—but I don't! I don't want to help her anymore! It didn't work! I want someone else to help her!" It felt like all the lava went into my words and rushed out of my mouth like I didn't care who got burned.

But no one jumped out of the way.

"I know this is a hard place to be in, Fiona, and I'm sorry," Mr. Rivera said very gently. "You don't have to talk to her. But Ms. Davis and I both think she might listen to you, if you want to tell her what you're feeling. Hearing your voice might make a difference."

"That's right," Ms. Davis said. "It's not easy, Fiona. But we're here for you. And I'm glad you've got a friend there to help, too."

Julia squeezed my hand again.

I squeezed back and took another breath. "What do I say?"

"Just speak your truth, like you did before," Ms. Davis said.

Mr. Rivera nodded. "Sometimes it takes a few times for the people we love to be able to hear us when they're struggling. All we can do is try our best."

"I need you to listen to me now, Fiona," Ms. Davis said. "There's no perfect way to do this. It's going to be messy, because life is messy. It might work, or it might not. That's not up to you. We just want you to have the chance to try, if you decide you want to. Got that?"

My throat was too full to speak, so I nodded.

"She's nodding yes," Julia said loudly. "And if she forgets, I can remind her."

"Thank you, Julia," Ms. Davis said. "I'm looking forward to meeting you one of these days. Fiona, any other questions before I finish talking to Mr. Rivera?"

"No," I managed to say.

Julia handed the phone to her dad. "She's definitely magic," she told me. "Witches can tell, you know."

And then Mr. Rivera was hanging up, asking me if I wanted to talk it through first, or if I was ready.

MS. DAVIS WAS RIGHT. IT WAS MESSY. WHEN MOM'S CURSE TRANS-forms her, she doesn't want to listen. Not when I told her I was fine here and I didn't want her to pick me up. Not when I asked her to stay where she was so they could help her. Not when I reminded her about her promise. She just talked and talked about how great things would be, and why wasn't I happy she was coming. She got louder and louder, until finally Julia grabbed the phone and told her to quit it, because I don't like yelling.

Mr. Rivera gave her a look, like maybe they were going to have a talk about grabbing people's phones later. But she didn't let go of my hand, and he didn't make her leave. And while my mom was quiet, I told her my biggest, scariest truth: that even if she came here to get me, I wasn't going home with her yet. I'd promised, and I was going to stay and do my part of our plan, even if she wouldn't do hers anymore.

Maybe those lava-words burned some of the bad-curse magic away, because she got quiet after that. I think she was cry-ing. My heart hurt, and my stomach hurt. Maybe I was crying, too.

"Sweetie, I miss you so much," she whispered.

"I miss you, too. But you have to do this, Mom." I took a deep, shuddery breath, along with Julia. "You have to stay there. I need you to."

I could hear her breathe with us,

too—in and out, ragged and broken, like a werewolf trying to remember what it feels like to be human. I'd almost given up when she sighed and said, "Fine."

Julia pumped her fist silently. Mr. Rivera just nodded, waiting.

I took another breath. "You'll stay there for the whole program? Promise?"

"I promise," she said. She sounded lost and lonely. But she sounded more like her real self.

Mr. Rivera gave me a thumbs-up and smiled. I thought of what Ms. Davis says, about things falling apart before they got better. My stomach didn't feel worse about this than it did about pretending everything was fine when it wasn't. I thought of something else Ms. Davis said, too.

"I love you, Mom," I told her.

"I love you, too, sweetie." I could definitely hear her crying now.

WHEN THAT WAS OVER, I LAY ON THE GRASS FOR A WHILE, STARING UP at the sky until my eyes stopped burning and just ached, while Julia pointed out the animals she could see in the clouds and Mr. Rivera called Ms. Davis and brought her up to date.

As soon as he got off the phone, Julia asked if we could all go get ice cream.

I didn't think I was ever going to want to eat anything again, but I didn't really want to be alone right then.

There was a long, long line, though. And somehow, as we stood there, the smell of warm waffle cones made my mind imagine what they might taste like. By the time it was our turn, I thought maybe I could at least try one. After all, I'd never had Blackberry Sunrise ice cream before.

22

MAYBE IT WAS the ice cream (which was delicious, even though it wasn't chocolate) or the warm sunshine. Or maybe it was the way Julia was telling me all about the book she was reading, like she was still my friend, even though she'd been there when things got messy. Maybe it was Mom's promise that she'd stay and get help, or my hope that maybe she'd keep this one. Whatever it was, I began to feel a little better.

Julia and I decided to continue on to the theater like we'd planned. I didn't want to miss the concert. Mr. Rivera had to do a few more things first, so he triple-checked that I was really okay with that, then let us go, so long as we saved him a seat.

Not many people were there yet. The seats sloped down toward the stage, so we got great ones way up at the back, where we could see and hear everything. The theater wasn't very big, but it had real seats that flipped up and down like the ones in a movie theater, instead of just rows of folding chairs.

"It's a lot like the talent show at my school," Julia said, examining the program. "Except there's an intermission in the middle. Some people are good, and some are terrible, but we all clap anyway."

I nodded. I felt worn out. But it was nice to sit there in the quiet theater while people slowly came in to find their seats. I let Julia's words wash over me.

"So what are you going to do with the rest of your summer?" Julia asked. "Now that you don't have to help your aunt and your great-uncle, I mean?"

"Um . . ." She was right, I realized. Aunt Becky and Annie didn't seem mad at each other now, and Great-Uncle Tim . . . well, he might still need some help, if he painted on other people's buildings again. But if that happened, I was calling Mr. Rivera. Even Great-Aunt Alta seemed happier now that she was playing her drums. It felt weird, like I didn't know what my job was anymore. "They'll probably need something else soon," I said, ignoring the wobble in my stomach. "Everyone needs something."

"Not me," Julia said cheerfully. "Well, okay, I have to eat and sleep and whatever. But I've got those covered. I mean, don't get me wrong—when you get your magic wand, I have a whole list of wishes! But I don't *need* anything."

I hadn't really thought about separating wishes out from needs like that before. "What would you wish for?" I asked. Maybe I didn't have my wand. But I'd finished Lessons 1 through 3. Maybe Lesson 4 would be about wishes instead?

"Right now? I wish I was up *there* tonight!" Julia pointed at the stage, her eyes shining.

I looked at the empty stage. "Like, doing a solo or something?"

"Nah. Someday, for sure—but not today. Too much work and too much practicing. But it would be fun to be part of someone else's entry—a backup dancer, maybe." She did a move in her seat and grinned. "I don't *need* to, though. It's just a wish. Maybe I'll sign up next year."

I nodded, still thinking.

When the theater lights grew dim, Mr. Rivera found us and took his seat.

"Everything okay?" I whispered.

He nodded and smiled, and I relaxed again.

As soon as it was really dark, Great-Aunt Alta swept out onto the stage in one of her long black witch dresses.

"Wow, she looks great!" Julia whispered.

I sat up and took a closer look. I'd never seen Great-Aunt Alta with her hair done up all fancy on top of her head. She was wearing black eye makeup and dark red lipstick. "Tonight, we are here to celebrate music in all its forms," she said, her voice booming. Everyone stopped rustling around and got quiet. "First up: Ms. Wood's youngest superstars, singing 'Let It Go.'"

A bunch of kindergarten-age kids filed out, herded along by a white lady with a tambourine, who nodded to Great-Aunt Alta. I wondered if the kids would be scared of her, but they didn't bat an eye as they wandered past, checking out the lights, waving to the audience, and poking each other. The lady rattled her tambourine, and the kids started singing. They were pretty bad, but probably not worse than the kindergarteners at my school. Some of them forgot the words, some of them had no idea what the tune was, and one of them kept twirling and jumping and crashing into his neighbors. They all got really into the parts they liked, so those were extra loud, and the rest was quiet.

But we all clapped a lot when they finally finished and took their bow. And then something I never could have imagined happened.

Great-Aunt Alta swept back onto the stage to announce the next group. And as the kids left, she knelt down, right there onstage, and gave each of them a high five as they ran off. They didn't seem scared of her at all.

I looked at Julia. Julia looked at me. "I didn't even know she knew what a high five was," I whispered.

Next was a grown-up band playing some old song about a stairway. It sounded like they were playing the same thing over and over, and a few times the singer just went "Oooooo" for a while. But we all clapped for them anyway, and Great-Aunt Alta gave them high fives, too. They didn't look scared of her, either.

After that, Great-Aunt Alta beckoned to someone off-stage, and a teenager all dressed in black ran out carrying a stool, and a couple more brought out a microphone and some other equipment. A Black guy came out carrying a guitar. He sat down on the stool, nodded to the audience, and started strumming his guitar and singing. His song was kind of sad and a little creepy, about a devil at the crossroads. It was great—like something right out of a story! Julia and I both whooped and shouted for him, and Great-Aunt Alta shook his hand as he left and said something to him we couldn't hear. Whatever it was made him smile.

There were two Asian teenagers who sang and tap-danced—Julia had a lot of thoughts about their performance—and a white lady in an old-fashioned dress who sang a sad song about dreams and waved her arms around way too much. That one took forever. But as far as I could tell, Great-Aunt Alta didn't say anything mean to any of them.

I was still thinking about Julia's wish while we waited in the bathroom line at intermission. "Do you really want to be a backup dancer?" I asked.

"Yeah!" she said. "Don't you?" She started doing robot moves.

I'd never really thought about it before. Maybe I'd get stage fright with everyone looking at me. But maybe not—

especially if I was performing with a friend. "I think I might have an idea," I said slowly.

"What kind of idea?" Julia switched from robot moves to snake moves (if snakes had wiggly arms).

"An idea for how to grant your wish, even without a wand," I said, doing a wiggly move of my own. "What if we were Great-Aunt Alta's backup dancers?"

Julia didn't answer. But her spinning jump and her shining eyes told me everything I needed to know. "Duh . . . duh . . . duh . . ." She made it super dramatic, waving her arms like she was a conductor. The lady in line behind us took a step back, but she was smiling.

"Duh-DUH! Boom, boom, boom, boom . . ." Julia shook her hips from side to side and grinned at me. "This is going to be *awesome*."

"She might say no," I warned.

"But she might say yes!" Julia pointed out, still smiling.

Considering how Great-Aunt Alta gave all those kids high fives, I thought Julia might be right.

WE LOOKED FOR HER DURING INTERMISSION, BUT WE COULDN'T FIND her. It didn't bother Julia. "We can sneak out during the song before hers and go backstage and ask her. At least we'll get to see what it's like behind the scenes, even if she says no," she said, grinning.

I'd never been backstage before. It made me a little

nervous. But it was kind of exciting, too. "Let's check once more and see if we can find her," I said.

So we searched until the lights flashed twice. But Great-Aunt Alta was nowhere to be found.

We climbed up the stairs to our seats, where Mr. Rivera was waiting. A bunch of teenagers in black clothes were setting up a drum set, some microphones, and a bunch of other equipment on the stage.

"Guess what, Dad? We're going to be famous!" Julia said, sliding into her seat.

I whispered my idea to Mr. Rivera as the theater lights went dark. "Do you think it's okay if we go back and ask her?"

Mr. Rivera grinned and gave us a thumbs-up just as Great-Aunt Alta swept out onto the stage. "Metal Death and the Revenants of Darkness," she said, her voice echoing out over the suddenly quiet audience.

Four figures in dark robes with their hoods up filed onto the stage. A little kid started to cry. Another one asked, "Are those Jawas?" really loudly before getting shushed. The figures pushed back their hoods, revealing four teenagers with pimply faces.

They walked over to their instruments. Then the one who was headed for the drum set looked at the audience, clutched his stomach, and ran off the stage.

"Come back here at once!" Great-Aunt Alta bellowed.

"Jeremy, you can do this!" She waited a moment. We could hear the sound of someone barfing loudly offstage, and Elfine's voice saying something soothing.

Great-Aunt Alta sighed. She put her microphone in its stand and stalked over to the drum set. She sat down on the stool and picked up the sticks.

"Uh, Ms. Starke?" The guitarist swallowed nervously. "Uh . . . I mean . . . I don't think . . ."

Great-Aunt Alta raised an eyebrow. "You don't think I could perform this song in my sleep? You didn't think I was listening to you when you rehearsed, young man?"

His face got red, and he went silent.

She looked straight at the audience. "The show must go on," she announced, and brought her sticks crashing down on the cymbals.

"Darkness!" she boomed into the drummer's microphone. The guitars and bass screeched and moaned, trying to catch up with her.

I honestly thought she was going to sing "No parents!" next, just like Lego Batman. But she didn't. She just pounded the drums like she was trying to outdo a thunderstorm.

I stared at Julia. Julia stared at me. We both grinned at the same time and looked at Mr. Rivera. He was staring, too. It was awesome.

Julia said afterward that they were playing heavy metal,

and that she thought it was supposed to sound all screechy like that, and that Great-Aunt Alta had probably even been pretty good. When she took her bow with the band at the end, she didn't smile, but she looked like maybe she would have, if it was a different kind of band and she wasn't acting like Lego Batman. Everyone clapped and cheered.

A bunch more people went after that, but honestly I can't really remember them. I was still getting over the shock of Great-Aunt Alta saving the day.

And then Julia was tugging on my sleeve. "It's time— let's go!"

My heart was pounding a little as I followed Julia out into the lobby and through a door marked BACKSTAGE. All around us, people were taking their costumes and makeup off, and talking about how they finally nailed that high part, and putting away sheets of music while tapping their toes. No wonder Great-Aunt Alta fit right in.

We found Great-Aunt Alta with the heavy-metal teenagers (even the one who barfed before). Aunt Becky was there, too—and Annie was with her! They weren't covered in frosting anymore. And Great-Uncle Tim was leaning against the wall, clutching his recorder in one hand and Renee's hand in the other. He didn't have handcuffs or a ball and chain or anything. He was staring at his shoes, but he was smiling. And Renee was smiling at him.

"Hello, Fiona— Ah, and your friend, too. Excellent,"

Great-Aunt Alta said. "Did you need something?" And she smiled, too.

I blinked and stared at her. It was like we'd traveled to some smiley parallel universe. She looked . . . kind of like Aunt Becky, actually. Or like the little girl in Great-Uncle Tim's comic.

For a minute, I didn't know what to say to this strange new Great-Aunt Alta. She already had everything she needed for her song. Maybe we should just go back to our seats.

But . . . I thought about Julia, making me have fun and having my back. It wouldn't hurt to ask about her wish, would it? Even if it did make me nervous?

I put my chin up, looked Great-Aunt Alta right in the eye, and spoke my truth. "I know your song is important to you. It's okay if you say no. But we wondered . . . Can we help you with it?"

"Yeah!" Julia said. "We're here to be your backup dancers!"

"I see," Great-Aunt Alta said, eyebrows raised.

I held my breath—and she smiled again. "You may have the area behind me and the drums in which to perform— stage right. Please refrain from bumping into the rest of the band. Any questions?"

I grinned and shook my head.

"Thank you for joining us," she said, still smiling.

And then it was time to go on. I never knew how bright the lights look from the stage. Honestly, I could hardly tell there was an audience out there at all. I couldn't see what steps Julia was doing or remember what she did before. But it didn't really matter, because I made up my own. (Besides, Great-Aunt Alta couldn't see us behind her and no one else really cared.) The stage vibrated with music, especially when Great-Aunt Alta really started pounding her drums, and Great-Uncle Tim and Aunt Becky and the teenagers were nodding together, rocking out in their own ways. Sometimes they even got some of the notes right, I think. When it was over, we all took a bow together and ran off.

And that was the end of the concert. Great-Aunt Alta thanked all the teenagers in black who'd set everything up, and the bake-sale people, and all the other volunteers, and then Elfine.

Elfine came out, carrying a huge bunch of dark red flowers. "Let's have a round of applause for Alta Starke, emcee extraordinaire and emergency musician of the evening!"

Great-Aunt Alta smiled again—three times in one day! Probably she saved them up all year, just for this. She swept a huge curtsy. As she rose, Elfine handed her the flowers. Julia took a picture for Clarice.

Dear Fiona,

Your mom asked me to let you know that she has a visiting day coming up. She misses you and would love to see you. But she understands that you might have a lot of feelings about all this, too.

I'm going to ask you to use what you've learned so far this summer to help yourself here. Show me what you've learned. Find your truth and speak it. (Or, you know— email it.) Think about your own story. Choose your own path. Your mom is doing what she needs to do. Now it's time to figure out what you want to do. It's okay to put that first.

What do you think? You don't have to, if you're not ready yet. There will be more opportunities.

Sincerely,
Nia Davis

Dear Ms. Davis,

Here's my truth: it might be hard for me to see her. Keeping my truth to myself wasn't working, but . . . I told her, and now I don't really know what else to say. And I know it's not going to be easy to leave her behind and come back here without her. Not because it's that bad here. (Well, unless you really don't like listening to someone practicing their drums all day long with their new band.) But she's still my mom. I don't want to say goodbye all over again.

Here's something I learned, though: even if we can't have our happily-ever-after yet, we should still try for our happily-for-now.

And seeing her would make me happy, even if it's not forever. I want to see her when I can, even though I know it might be hard, too. I miss her so much.

Your apprentice,
Fiona

P.S. Guess what?! I granted a wish! See, my friend Julia didn't need anything, but she wished she could be a backup dancer, and . . . Here's a picture of us that Mr. Rivera sent me. Yes, that's really us! It was awesome.

Dear Mom,

I want to come see you. I want to hear how you're doing and what you're learning there. And I want to tell you what I've been doing, too. I don't know if you were paying attention before, but I made a friend here. We hung out at this festival they have in town and did all kinds of stuff I've never done before. I really miss you, and I still want to go home when you finish your program. But I'm having fun here, too, for now. Sometimes it feels all mixed up. But I've decided to enjoy the parts I can anyway.

Aunt Becky says I can bring you a whole box of stuff from her bakery, including the new coconut cupcakes she and her friend Annie are making together. And Great-Uncle Tim is teaching me how to draw a dragon for the card I'm making you.

Love,
Fiona

P.S. Here are some pictures from the festival that my friend Julia and her dad sent me. I'm the tall chicken with the black-and-white feathers. That's me and Julia, with our chalk drawings, and Hula-Hooping, and with Buttercup the alpaca. And yes, that really is me onstage doing a backup dance. Doesn't Great-Aunt Alta look amazing?! And don't I look amazing, too?! Bet you never knew I could do that!

P.P.S. We have to come back here next year for a visit, so I can help out at the festival again and so you can see it all, too. Great-Aunt Alta decided it's a tradition. Traditions matter a lot to her. (Besides, I want to see Julia again.)

P.P.P.S. I'm sending you my biggest hug. Next week, I'll give you another one in person! I can't wait.

ACKNOWLEDGMENTS

Stories don't grow in vacuums. Thank you to all the bakers, artists, musicians, helpers, readers, small-town residents, and lovers of fairy tales who gave this book its magic. Thank you to Brenna Shanks, for that conversation about how Stella Gibbons's *Cold Comfort Farm* is not a Cinderella story; it set my mind humming (along with Lynne Truss's introduction to the edition I have). Thank you to Natalie Lloyd for the Blackberry Sunrise ice cream, and to Ursula Vernon for some of my favorite comfort reads.

Thank you to Caroline Stevermer, Jen Adam, Edith Hope Bishop, Alene Moroni, Melissa Koosmann, Liz Wong, Will Taylor, Kim Baker, Marin Younker, Mike Denton, Sarah Hunt, Lish McBride, Brenda Winter Hansen, Alison Weatherby, Courtney Gould, Gillian Allen, Jenny Scott Tynes, Rae Rose, Preeti Gopalan, Elizabeth Goode, and my Emerald City Literary Agency and SCBWI Western

Washington friends and colleagues, who listen to my ups and downs, keep me writing, and remind me to take breaks.

Thank you to Artie Bennett, Alison Kolani, Amy Schroeder, Jim Armstrong, Kayla Overbey, Jake Eldred, Shaughnessy Miller, Deanna Meyerhoff, Lisa Nadel, Kristin Schulz, Adrienne Waintraub, Anna Bernstein, Jasmine Walls, Barbara Brainin, Kamalii Yeh Garcia, and everyone who helped me make this book truer and more magical, richer and deeper, and who connect readers with my books. And an extra-special thank-you to the booksellers, teachers, and librarians who share their love of stories with young readers.

Thank you to Mandy Hubbard and Nancy Siscoe, who believed in this story immediately, to Marisa DiNovis, who kept us rolling, to Taryn Fagerness, who brings my stories to far-off lands, and to Michelle Cunningham and Jen Valero, who swirled it all together so beautifully.

Thank you to Kelly Murphy for bringing Fiona's imagination to life (and for my very first map!).

My deepest thanks to all who shared their personal stories in the hopes that they'd make someone else's path easier, and who listened to my stories, too. Thank you to those who taught me how to be a better helper (and how to help myself, too).

Thank you to Eric, whose daily support lets me dive deeper and go farther (and who finds my trail of cold tea mugs).

Finally, thank you to my family, there from the beginning and found along the way. I love you.